Geoffrey Trease was born and brought up in Nottingham, near Sherwood Forest. So it's not surprising that history was his favourite subject at school or that his first novel, *Bows Against the Barons* (1934), should have been all about Robin Hood. Since then he has written numerous adventure novels for young people – many of them historical – as well as mystery stories, adult novels, plays, biographies and other works of non-fiction.

*Calabrian Quest* is Geoffrey Trease's one hundredth book. Like his ninety-ninth, *Shadow Under the Sea* (also published by Walker), it's an exciting mystery tale set in the present day. The setting is Italy and the book's cast of colourful characters includes a biker priest and a local Mafia boss. "I'm very fond of Italy, having been there a number of times," says the author. "It's a favourite topic of mine." The country has featured in a number of his books, including *Follow My Black Plume*, *A Thousand for Sicily* and *The Arpino Assignment*.

Now in his eighties, Geoffrey Trease continues to write with the same energy and excitement as when he first started. "I have a completely adult attitude to historic accuracy," he says, "but I have a child's enjoyment of a secret passage or galloping horses at midnight. You've got to believe it all yourself and it thrills me immensely."

## Also by Geoffrey Trease

# CALABRIAN QUEST

## GEOFFREY TREASE

First published 1990 by Walker Books Ltd
87 Vauxhall Walk. London SE11 5HJ

This edition published 1992, 1993

© 1990 Geoffrey Trease

Printed and bound in Great Britain by
Cox and Wyman Ltd, Reading, Berkshire

British Library Cataloguing in Publication Data
A catalogue record for this title is available
from the British Library

ISBN 0-7445-2304-4

## Author's Note

Alaric's hidden grave is real history, but I have taken a few imaginative liberties with the geography of the Cosenza district, for it is many years since I was there.

# PROLOGUE

For those few minutes – winded, eyes and mouth gritty with dust, scrabbling in the loose earth of the crater – Paul thought this was the finish. He was done for.

As his head cleared after the explosion he became less pessimistic. He was not bleeding. He felt no pain. That wasn't always a good sign, though. You might be paralysed from the waist down. You could have had both legs blown off.

In panic he moved his legs. They were there. His fingers felt something hard, like a pencil. He held on to it. He raised his head, then froze again, sprawled across the tumbled earth, as another plane swooped, its machine-gun chattering. *Ratatatatat* . . . He heard the crump of a bomb. A tawny haze drifted overhead.

This is one hell of a way to celebrate a nineteenth birthday, he thought. What hopes of seeing a twentieth?

The day had started so well. No resistance. The Nazis pulling out so fast, even the forward patrols couldn't make contact with them. The Eighth Army was going through southern Italy like a hot knife through butter. No opposition. Only booby-traps and blown bridges.

Ten minutes ago this valley had looked peaceful enough. They had splashed through the boulder-strewn river, scarcely knee-deep after the dry summer, no problem.

The village, facing them from the hillside, a jumble of beige walls and terracotta tiles, had looked innocent enough. Until last week – in Sicily or North Africa – they'd have approached with caution, ready for a murderous burst of fire. But the enemy seemed to have given up defending such places.

White flags fluttered. Two little dark-faced girls waved excitedly. A donkey grazed. A boy herded goats. He yelled a welcome across the fields.

Then the dive-bombers roared down, the swastikas black on their wings. They screeched along the narrow band of sky, level with the crinkled ridges either side. No time to dive for cover under the olive-trees. Paul remembered only the first explosion, one of his friends tossed like a rag doll – and regaining consciousness in that vast hole gouged out of the flat field.

He conquered his impulse to struggle to his feet and race for shelter. The planes might come back. Safer to lie absolutely still, his khaki battle-dress blending with the sandy earth. Warily he peeped up at the village. He hoped the little girls had run indoors.

The village seemed untouched. There was a church at the top. Higher still, outlined against the vivid blue, was a cross. A wayside calvary like those in Sicily, where peasants would pause, cross themselves, and mutter a prayer. To Paul it was a reminder to thank God that he was alive.

He was still clutching the object in his hand. It was mud-coated, lumpy at one end, but as he pressed the lump the dried mud crumbled away, leaving a spoonlike oval of tarnished metal.

It *was* a spoon, but not like any spoon he had ever seen. Narrow and straight, ending in a point, not broadening into a handle. As he scratched at the oval end, the ingrained soil flaking away under his fingernail, he saw lettering incised in the blackened metal, but he could not read it.

Afterwards he reckoned that the bomb must have landed in a rubbish dump, which would account for the various objects he had glimpsed protruding from the heap. But the sergeant was bawling, and they all had to jump up and race for the shelter of the buildings as more planes came screeching down.

*Wheeee . . . whoosh!*

Looking back, Paul saw that one of the bombs had obliterated the very crater in which he had lain. He had got out just in time.

That night he found he still had the old spoon in his pocket. Though it looked neither beautiful nor valuable he kept it for luck.

Later, when a wound sent him to hospital in Naples, he showed it to an army chaplain visiting the wards.

It was silver all right. A friendly nurse had cleaned it till it shone. There *was* some lettering. *PAVLVS VIVAS.*

"Latin," said the chaplain. "'Long may you live, Paulus!' They used the same letter for V and U. A baby's christening spoon."

"Paulus? Well, what d'ye know? I guess it really *was* meant. My lucky day."

The chaplain glanced at the name on his bed,

*Vandyke P.* "You mean you're a Paul yourself?" He laughed. "Better your name on this than on the bomb!"

"I guess I'll keep this just as long as I live."

Paul did. Nearly half a century later the memory of finding it was to come back to him with a rush.

# ONE

I wish something interesting would happen, Karen thought, as she led her little party up the curving stairs.

This, with luck, would be the last party of visitors before they closed. Only five: an elderly American couple with a bespectacled grandson silent at their heels, and a tired young mother, gleaming with perspiration, dragging a fractious child.

Often Karen wished she had taken that other vacation job in the wine-bar. It would have been much livelier. But Andy had argued that the experience here would be useful if she was really set on a career in museums. His uncle owned the Manor. Andy himself had promised to help out for a few weeks.

"This is the grand drawing-room," she announced as the party reached the first doorway. "You will notice the Chinese wallpaper. It was just coming into fashion at this period."

It made a change when someone asked a question – provided that she knew the answer. Usually she did. This party didn't look as if it included any experts. They stared round politely. The old gentleman murmured "Mighty interestin' " at intervals. Karen kept her eye on the restless child, a little boy, lest he duck under the protective ropes to bounce on the exquisite sofas.

They moved on. "This next room," she

announced brightly, "is known as 'Sir Harry's Study'. He was the third baronet. He made the Grand Tour of Italy in 1782. On the table you see some of the interesting mementoes he brought back."

They shuffled in behind her. The American lady cast a critical eye on a gloomy oil painting.

"The Doge's Palace," said Karen helpfully. "Venetian."

"So I see, my dear." The lady's tone was icy. "I guess this Sir Harry hadn't much taste in art."

Karen wouldn't argue about that. "It's no Canaletto," she agreed. Better let the old witch realize that she did know *something* about painters. "The next picture—"

"Thank you, my dear. I think we'd prefer just to look round quietly for ourselves."

"Of course . . . Madam," Karen added hastily.

Most likely this expensive-looking lady had been touring Italy for the past half-century and knew it backwards. Karen herself had never been nearer Venice than a pizza parlour in London. Never mind, she thought, soon set that right. Roll on August. She'd be on her way with Andy and the others. Why else was she doing this job?

The visitors moved round, mumbling comments on the pictures, the statuettes, the table laid out with labelled curiosities Sir Harry had picked up. A carnival mask, a murderous stiletto, an ivory fan, a chunk of lava from Vesuvius . . . He had not been a systematic collector.

A notice said PLEASE DO NOT TOUCH. A thick red cord kept people from getting too close. But

12

you couldn't be too careful with children. She must watch the boy. At least he couldn't grab that ghastly dagger. It was firmly sticky-taped to the table. "Has anyone any questions?" she said. They all looked glassy-eyed and dopey with the heat.

The young mother, however, came hurrying across. Karen put on her most obliging smile. One question.

"He wants the toilet! Could you tell me . . . ?"

Well, I asked for that, thought Karen ruefully. Aloud she said: "Of course. I'll show you."

It had been impressed on her by Andy's uncle that you never, *never* left your party unattended. But you couldn't be in two places at once. The Americans looked honest.

She led the way along the landing. "Through that archway – see? Door on the right."

"Thanks ever so!"

"You're welcome."

Ten minutes ago she'd been thinking, I wish something interesting would happen. Now suddenly it did. There was an outburst of voices from Sir Harry's Study.

"You mustn't *do* that!"

"I only wanted a peek at it—"

"*Paul!*" That was the imperious old lady.

"Hell! The darned thing's stuck down!"

That last cry, from the husband, fully alerted Karen. The harmless-looking old gentleman had laid unlawful hands on one of the exhibits.

She seized the whistle that dangled unseen inside her shirt. Every guide carried one. Sir Peter had made the rule: anything suspicious, anything

13

you can't handle alone, blow your whistle and stand there till help arrives.

So, as she reached the doorway and saw the old man reaching across to the table, she blew a piercing blast. Afterwards, Andy said she'd panicked. But his uncle had backed her up. Better too much zeal than act too late.

The effect of that blast was paralysing.

The elderly gentleman turned in horrified embarrassment. He had one long leg over the red cord and was fumbling with one of the exhibits. To Karen's relief it was not the stiletto but an ancient Roman spoon. Like the dagger, it was sticky-taped to the table to deter pilferers.

"I – I must apologize, young lady—"

"Leave this to me, Paul!" The lady advanced with dignity upon Karen, who had posted herself by the door, ready to bar the way – or to escape if the visitors became violent. "I hope, young woman, you do not take us for criminals? Blowing your whistle in that melodramatic manner!"

"I was obeying instructions," said Karen with spirit. "I'm afraid this gentleman wasn't." She faced him, softening. He looked so painfully guilty. "You're not supposed to go behind the rope."

"I sure am sorry, my dear. It was seeing that spoon. I guess I forgot myself."

He was really rather a nice old boy. She wished she hadn't blown her whistle. There must be an innocent explanation.

His wife had drawn the bespectacled youth aside and was instructing him in an emphatic undertone.

"You got your wallet, Maxie?"

"Sure. But . . . I don't think . . . really—"

"You just do what I say!"

"Don't you think Grandfather himself—"

"You know he never carries *money*. And you can't handle this sorta situation with a credit card. Let's see what you've got." Karen heard the rustle of notes. "A five should fix it. Go right ahead, Maxie boy."

Oh, horrors, thought Karen. He was coming towards her, crimson-faced and sweating. It hadn't been *his* fault. She felt sorry for him.

"Please, there's no need." She pushed away his furtive hand. "It was just a misunderstanding, I'm sure . . ."

Tips were OK. But not *bribes*!

She heard running footsteps. Andy burst in, eager for action, disappointed when he saw the weakness of the opposition. His uncle followed at a more dignified pace. The mother and child chose that moment to return. The room was suddenly crowded.

"What's the trouble?" Sir Peter was unruffled.

"False alarm," said Karen quickly. "This gentleman—"

But the American spoke for himself. Now that he had straightened up to his full height he looked rather distinguished. "This old spoon here." He pointed. "I got one like it back home. Found it in a bomb crater in Italy."

"Ah," said Sir Peter amiably. "You were there in the war?"

"I'll say! North Africa, Sicily, Italy—"

"Like my father."

"You don't say!"

The two men were at once on the best of terms. The American continued: "My spoon's got some wording. A padre told me it meant 'wishing you long life, Paul'. And my own name being Paul, I've kept that old spoon like a lucky charm. So naturally I wondered if there was any inscription on *your* spoon. Guess I should've asked this young lady—"

"I think it's on the card," Karen said and pointed. She read the faded handwriting. "*Roman christening spoon, 4th cent. AD. Inscribed, VIVAS PAVLINA.*"

The American's delight was dramatic. "Well, what d'ye know? This one's for a girl Paulina!"

"Twins," suggested Andy.

Sir Peter detached the card and offered it to the visitor for easier examination. The old gentleman's excitement grew.

"Look, it says, *Reverse: Christian monogram XP*! My spoon's got that same 'XP'. Don't know who this guy was, but those spoons must be a pair. And it says, '*from S. Italy*' – so was mine!"

"There's rather a lot of southern Italy," said Sir Peter mildly.

"You're telling *me*, sir. I footslogged every darned mile of it, right the way up to Naples. But there are the initials, remember – XP on both of them."

It seemed a shame to spoil his triumph, but Karen had to say: "You'll find those letters on lots of silver from this period. Actually they aren't XP

– they're in the Greek alphabet. The X stands for Greek 'CH', as in 'chorus'. And the P is a Greek 'R'.

"You don't say! You know Greek then?"

"Only the alphabet. These two Greek letters make our three, C, H, R – short for 'Christ'. So they're found on most Christian silver."

The old gentleman looked crestfallen but recovered quickly. "I still reckon those spoons belong together. Paul and Paulina, twins, like our young friend said."

His wife glanced at her watch. "We must be getting along. I don't suppose—" She turned to Sir Peter. "I'm afraid I don't know your name."

"Wakefield. Peter Wakefield."

"I don't suppose, Mr Wakefield, you'd consider an offer for this spoon of yours?"

The baronet's smile remained urbane. Karen noted with interest that he had not disclosed his title. "I'm *so* sorry, madam. We have to keep the collection together."

The lady did not look as though she was used to being denied, least of all when offering good money. She fumbled in her bag, but mercifully produced only a card. "Well, if you should ever change your mind – Vandyke's the name." She laughed. "Birthdays are *such* a problem. Especially for the man who has everything."

Her grandson had flushed hotly again. Karen pitied him.

Downstairs a bell jangled for closing time. "But you must finish your tour of the house," said Sir Peter.

17

"Thanks – but I guess we'd better get back to our hotel."

The mother and child seemed more than ready to end their visit, so they all went down together, Mr Vandyke explaining how he had picked up his own spoon in a bomb crater, under fire. "I'd a hunch there was some other stuff lying around, but it wasn't the moment to go looking."

"You never went back to the place?" asked Andy.

The two men burst out laughing. Sir Peter recalled his own father's memories of that whirlwind advance.

At the front door, there were cordial farewells all round. Although Mr Vandyke was supposed never to carry money on him, Karen felt something pressed discreetly into her hand.

Over dinner Andy said: "You were a bit unkind to him."

"Unkind?"

"Squashing his theory that both spoons belonged to an unknown guy with the initials XP!"

"Historical truth is sacred," she said primly. "Like scientific truth." Andy loved arguing, but she always stood up to him.

"Pity old Harry wasn't keener on accuracy," said Sir Peter. "He should have said exactly where he found *his* spoon."

"Perhaps he did," said Andy's aunt, "in that journal he kept of his tour."

"*That* interminable screed?" Sir Peter turned to Karen. "My poor ancestor knew no more about writing than he did about painting. It's *the* most boring hotchpotch of travel impressions—"

"It's there in the library," said Lady Wakefield. "They can judge for themselves."

After the meal they found it and turned its rustling pages, poring over the spidery brown handwriting, tracing Sir Harry's journey south from Naples. He was not an inspiring writer. He had stared at the obvious places and recorded his equally obvious impressions. But after a few minutes Andy let out a cry of satisfaction.

*Cosenza,* Sir Harry had written, *a wretched town, fever-stricken, the inn filthy and full of fleas. Bought an antique spoon from peasant who found it in field. Rogue swore it was Roman. According to Mr Gibbon's book it was in Calabria, at Cosenza, that Alaric, King of the Goths, died and was buried with his plunder from the sack of Rome. To this day none of it has been found.*

"Interesting," said Andy.

"Very."

They both spoke casually, but the look in his eyes told her that the same thought had occurred to him as to herself.

"Gibbon," she said. "The man who wrote *Decline and Fall of the Roman Empire.*" She gazed round the tall bookshelves. "Would it be here?"

"Sure to be. No gentleman's library complete without!"

They located it on a top shelf and quailed at the sight of the six leather-bound old volumes. But Andy was not to be deterred. He found the library

19

ladder and perched on it precariously, taking out one volume after another, showering dust on to Karen's newly washed hair. "When did he die," he called down, "this Alaric bloke?"

"I think Rome was sacked in AD 410."

"This should be the volume, then." He came down and opened it on the table. They soon found the passage in chapter thirty-one. "Consentia," he said.

"That'll be the old Latin name. Cosenza now."

They read it together, in the stately eighteenth-century prose. *The ferocious character of the barbarians was displayed in the funeral of a hero whose valour and fortune they celebrated with mournful applause. By the labour of a captive multitude they forcibly diverted the course of the Busentinus, a small river that washes the walls of Consentia. The royal sepulchre, adorned with splendid spoils and trophies of Rome, was constructed in the vacant bed; the waters were then restored to their natural channel—*

"Wow!" gasped Karen, as she got the idea.

*—and the secret spot where the remains of Alaric had been deposited was for ever concealed by the inhuman massacre of the prisoners who had been employed to execute the work.*

Karen shuddered. "How ghastly!"

"Worse things happened under Hitler and Stalin." Andy jumped to his feet. "The point is – if that treasure never *was* found, it's still there in Calabria. Where are those Americans staying tonight?"

"I think they said the Feathers."

"Come on then. We'll run down on our bikes. They may be off in the morning. We'd better catch them now."

# TWO

The hotel dinner had been leisurely and luxurious. Though Grandma said she loved the simple little country places she had a sure nose, thought Max, for good food.

He was thankful to escape from the dimly-lit dining-room and the dim elderly voices. He slipped into the flower-scented garden, now aglow with sunset.

He was enjoying this first trip to Britain and grateful to his grandparents for bringing him. Only . . . he wished they'd realize he'd grown up lately. He wasn't a kid to be fussed over all the time. Grandma ought to let him off the lead now and then.

Four young people – they looked about eighteen, like himself – disappeared through a doorway marked "Public Bar". From the laughter within he guessed that this was where the action would be found. He'd heard about the English pubs, where you could talk to strangers and make friends. Pubs here were the centre of life, like cafés in Paris.

Mastering his natural shyness, he headed for that cheerful door. But a waiter appeared at his elbow.

"Excuse me, sir. Mrs Vandyke is asking for you. I've just taken the coffee into the lounge."

Max knew what that meant. No escape. He could only pray that Grandma would get talking with some of the other guests. Then, while she was holding forth, he'd swallow his coffee and quietly fade from the scene.

His grandfather was on the settee beside her, sipping his whiskey. He said coffee at night kept him awake. Max had a suspicion that he'd have enjoyed his Bourbon more if he'd gone into the bar for it. What Grandfather liked most on these trips abroad was becoming a nobody. To get away from the telephones and the army of secretaries and advisers and executives and fund-raisers, not to be treated as *important*, to drive himself, not sit behind a chauffeur – that was his real idea of a vacation. But to slip away into the public bar . . . No. Grandma would have thought that "unsuitable". And, big man though Paul Vandyke was reckoned in the business world, he was the meekest of husbands.

"Ah, Maxie boy!" said Grandma. "Thought we'd lost you."

"Just wanted a breath of air."

"You got to watch these summer evenings. Easy to catch a chill. Don't want you laid up somewheres."

"I'll be careful." He stifled his irritation.

Was it going to be another of those evenings? Would she go over his future again? Lecture him on the importance of this, the danger of that, and the need to make "useful" friendships?

Deliverance came from an unexpected quarter. The waiter returned and murmured to his grandfather. Max caught the surprised exclamation. "Asking for *me*? A young couple?" Who could

23

have tracked him down in this remote village?

"From the Manor, sir. A Mr Wakefield. I believe he is Sir Peter's nephew."

The word "Sir" alerted Mrs Vandyke. "Then you'd best show them in."

"Very good, madam."

The Wakefield youth came striding across to them. Behind him, Max saw with mixed feelings that breath-taking girl Grandma had expected him to bribe. He had hoped in his embarrassment never to see her again. Or did he mean that he had not hoped ever to see her again?

His feelings sure *were* mixed, he realized. Tonight she did not look as alarming as when she had blown her whistle and blocked the doorway. In fact she looked – but what was the use of finding words to describe how she looked? She must be Wakefield's girlfriend.

"We do apologize for troubling you," began their visitor smoothly.

Grandma's answer was smooth too, but with the smoothness of ice. "I trust you have not found any valuables missing?"

Max felt for him. Grandma could be a devil. But this Wakefield could hold his own. "Oh, certainly not! That *was* an unfortunate misunderstanding, wasn't it?"

"Sit down," said Grandfather warmly. "What'll you drink?"

"They will drink coffee – like us," said Grandma swiftly. "Maxie, ring the bell. There – on the wall!"

Max sprang to obey. With Grandma it was best

to spring. When he got back, the girl had been waved into his vacated seat. He pulled up another beside her. She'd scarcely opened her mouth yet. She hadn't had much chance.

Wakefield was explaining why they'd come. "We were checking up on those two spoons. *Our* spoon . . ." He hesitated. Then he went on carefully, "We wondered if you could tell us, sir, where you found *your* spoon?"

Max noted how he'd rephrased his question. He began to revise his idea that this was just a bone-headed, upper-class young Englishman. He'd make a better businessman than I ever will, thought Max, if I live to be a hundred. It had never been his own ambition to be a businessman – just everyone else's.

Grandfather's face was a study in wrinkled concentration. Was *he* being cagey too? Folks said you had to get up early to outsmart Paul Vandyke. But why should he hold back any information he had? Most likely he was genuinely foxed. It had all been about fifty years ago.

"You got me there, young man," he admitted. "We were moving so fast. I didn't have a map – only the officers had maps. I know there was some town in Calabria we were trying to by-pass – can't remember the name. The Germans had taken down all the road-signs. My company was sent to outflank this place, in case they'd mined the bridge. So we had to go up the valley some way—"

"And cross the river? You mentioned a river this afternoon."

25

"Sure. It was just after that the dive-bombers caught us. That bit I do remember." Grandfather chuckled grimly. "That's where I found my spoon."

His memory was coming back. Max had never heard this story in full. Now he could almost see the white flags flapping over the rooftops, the little girls waving, the tall crucifix silhouetted against the sky . . . Then the skimming shadows of the enemy planes, the blinding dust and fumes from the exploding bombs . . .

He stole a glance at the girl, Karen. Her fingers were moving on her lap. She seemed, very stealthily, to be writing. Just a word or two at intervals. She had no paper. She was writing as a child might in school, on her own bare wrist, pressing the ballpoint on to her taut skin.

Max was intrigued. Like her boyfriend, if that's what he was, she seemed remarkably interested in this coincidence of the spoons.

"You don't remember the name of the river, sir?" Wakefield was certainly persistent.

"I guess not. I'm real sorry."

The English boy hesitated. To Max his thought-processes were almost visible. With obvious reluctance, almost desperation, he plunged.

"The town wouldn't be – Cosenza?"

"Cosenza!" Grandfather echoed the name triumphantly. "That was it. Yes, Cosenza!"

Grandma had kept silent all this time, contenting herself with pouring fresh coffee. "Is that where your ancestor got *his* spoon?"

"Yes, Mrs Vandyke. Quite a coincidence, really."

"It certainly is. And considering my husband had this notion there were other things lying around, valuable things maybe . . ." She paused significantly.

Grandfather let out one of his deep-chested laughs. "Bit late now to go back for another look!"

"I should think so," said Grandma disdainfully. Max knew exactly what she was thinking: we Vandykes don't have to go grubbing about for valuables, we've got all the money we need, and more. To his relief she did not say so.

"It would be pretty difficult now to pin-point where that crater was," said Wakefield.

Grandfather nodded. "Impossible, I'd say. I told you, another bomb landed on it – there were lots of bombs."

The girl broke silence. "It might just be worth taking a peek round – if one happened to be in the neighbourhood."

Was it imagination – or did her friend seem a bit put out by her remark? If he was, he recovered instantly.

"To be perfectly frank, Mr Vandyke, *we* may happen to 'be in the neighbourhood' in a week or two—"

"*We?*" Grandma could cut across any conversation with one word – most effectively.

"Karen and I. We've got Inter-Rail tickets we're making a month's tour of Europe—"

"*Alone?*" Another of Grandma's block-busting one-worders. Max squirmed.

"Well, you're not alone much in trains and hostels—"

Karen spoke again. Her tone wasn't smooth like her friend's. She hadn't taken to Grandma.

"Mrs Vandyke means, are we going by ourselves?" She faced Grandma, with an effort to be polite but clearly bristling. "We're going as a foursome. My cousin Julie – she's over here for a year from Australia. And Chris, Andy's friend at college." She stopped, tight-lipped, as if to say, I hope your curiosity is satisfied.

"How very interesting," said Grandma blandly. Then Grandfather charged helpfully into the strained silence, asking questions about student travel abroad.

Andy explained about tickets. They gave you unlimited travel over the European railway system for one month. With economical meals and accommodation it was a marvellously cheap way to see the world.

Max listened enviously. It sounded more fun than Grandma's mode of travel, all airports, hired cars, and first-class hotels. He ventured a question of his own, but Grandma brushed him out of the conversation like a fly.

"It wouldn't suit *you*, Maxie. And in your case, fortunately, there's no need."

No need. Her favourite phrase. If you had enough dollars there was no sense in taking chances, risking discomfort, having unexpected misadventures. You were sensible. You did nothing, ever, to make your family anxious.

"And you figured all along on going to Italy?" asked Grandfather.

"Oh, yes! That was a 'must' from the start.

Karen's doing Art History for her degree—"

"You will want to see all those wonderful galleries, my dear," said Grandma kindly, making it clear that she had seen them all herself, many times.

Karen agreed. But she also wanted to see the temples and mosaics in Sicily. She looked pleased when Grandma had to confess she had never been there, not liking the Mafia and their kidnapping habits.

"We can go all the way by train," said Andy. "There's a rail ferry across the Straits of Messina. Actually, the line passes quite close to Cosenza. We might stop off, just out of curiosity." He was trying to sound casual.

"Why not?" Grandfather fished out one of his cards and passed it over. "And if you *should* find out anything about those spoons – million to one against, I know—"

"We'll write and tell you," the girl promised.

It was time to be going. Max and his grandfather went out with them. They had bicycles propped against the wall outside.

"If I should remember anything more," said Grandfather, "I can ring you at the Manor?"

"For two more weeks, then we're off."

Good-nights were said. The English couple switched on their lamps and sped off into the darkness.

"Nice young people," said Grandfather. "Don't suppose we'll ever clap eyes on 'em again."

"No," Max agreed, and felt a pang in saying it.

# THREE

They could not talk as they sped down the winding road in single file, the hedges reeling back in the wavering whiteness of their lights. Only when they had stowed their machines in the stables and were crossing the cobbled yard could Andy ask: "What did you think of the grandson?"

"Not much. He lets her walk all over him."

"She'd take some stopping." Andy sounded half admiring. "What a dragon! I was sorry for Maxie. Quite liked him. What's wrong with him?"

"Oh, I don't know." They went through the back door, past the butler's pantry, where there'd been no butler for years. She was faintly irritated. She said: "His hair's too short and tidy. He was wearing a *suit*. And a *tie*. He looked middle-aged!"

Andy laughed tolerantly. "I expect Grandma puts years on him. Anything else upset you?"

"I didn't notice him that much."

"Only his hair, his tie, his suit, and – shall we say – his polite deference to his aged grandparents?" Andy could never resist teasing her.

"I'm just not used to mixing with the filthy rich," she said shortly.

He almost hooted with delight. "There we go again! The old fierce pride in your honest working-class origins. The wickedness of wealth and privilege—"

"Oh, shut up. I'm not like that." He was always going on about what he called her "inverted snobbery" – not looking *up* to the rich and titled as "better" than oneself (which was absurd) but automatically looking *down* on them if they didn't live in a council house and carry a union card. You should treat them on their personal merits, Andy argued.

She agreed with him, really. It was logical. But you couldn't help your instincts and your upbringing. Mrs Vandyke had got right up her nose.

Alone in her bedroom she remembered, before she washed, to copy into her notebook a summary of those inky jottings she had made on her wrist.

*They had crossed the river. About 100 yds on. N. side. Church in front. Cross on hillside just above.*

If they ever did get to this place they could work out roughly where that bomb-crater had been, even if it was flat now. The church should still be there, even if it had been rebuilt. If the wayside cross had been demolished, the pious peasants would surely have put up another. If they lined up those two landmarks and walked forward they'd be sure to pass over the spot where Mr Vandyke had found his spoon.

There was one snag. Anything that was part of King Alaric's treasure should be in the bed of the river, not a hundred yards from the bank. There was an answer to that. Rivers could change their courses, more than once maybe, in nearly sixteen hundred years. Andy would know all about that from his geology.

A more serious snag cropped up next day at breakfast.

Andy's uncle and aunt listened with interest to their account of the previous evening. Sir Peter gave Andy a shrewd look. "And Mr Vandyke found *his* spoon near Cosenza?"

"He said so."

"So, after all, he did remember the name?"

"With a bit of prompting," said Karen.

"Ah! Was he just anxious to please, d'you think?"

"He seemed pretty positive," Andy said.

Karen came to his support. "He was emphatic, once the name came back to him. Don't you believe him, Sir Peter?"

She never minded calling him Sir Peter. It was his name and, while she was on this guide job, he was her boss. He was nice, not "filthy" rich, certainly not "idle" rich. He worked as hard as anyone, keeping this lovely place going for everyone to enjoy.

He smiled at her now across the table. "One thing puzzles me. I know something about this Italian campaign. My father went through it all." He stood up. "I'll just check something in the library."

He was soon back, his finger in an open book, his manner a blend of triumph and apology. Triumph because he was right, apology because it would disappoint them.

"As I feared – no American troops went near Cosenza." He laid down the book, open at a map of southern Italy with bold black arrows and dates marking the Allied advances. Andy and Karen craned over eagerly.

"Cosenza," she muttered, spotting the name "Oh!"

The map left no room for doubt. It was the British Eighth Army, the famous "Desert Rats" from North Africa, which had crossed the narrow straits from Sicily and swept northwards through Calabria from the toe of Italy.

"The Yanks landed much higher up the coast." Sir Peter pointed to a black arrow near Naples. "The Fifth Army, under their General Clark. Mr Vandyke must have got muddled in his geography. They weren't within hundreds of miles of Cosenza. They were never in Calabria at all. He must have found his spoon much further north."

Their wild dream of a treasure-hunt was exploded like a pricked balloon. No one could argue with that map. Just then the telephone interrupted with its old-fashioned strident ring.

Sir Peter crossed to the side table. "Who? Oh, you want my nephew. Hang on. For you, Andy. Your friend Chris."

"At this time of day?" Andy looked startled. Karen felt a spasm of alarm. She and her friends tried to keep phone calls to the cheap evening period.

She caught the word "hospital". Then Andy's relieved tone, "Oh, not you. Thank God for that."

She shared his relief. She had dreaded some accident to Chris, his motorbike probably . . . But Andy's tone continued serious.

"Oh, your father? I *am* sorry." He listened –

Karen caught the faint rustle of a distant explanation. "No, no," said Andy, "don't worry about
*us*. We quite understand. You couldn't possibly
. . . at a time like this . . . Lord no, *we'll* fix something. Karen sends her love . . ." He looked at her
and she nodded vigorously. "We'll be in touch.
Fingers crossed! Bye!"

"He can't come with us?" Her voice was
strained.

"'Fraid not. His dad's been rushed to hospital.
Tests, then maybe an operation. Sounds a bit
sinister."

"Oh, *poor* Chris! *And* his mum."

"He wanted to let us know at once. He's got to
stick around – he obviously can't go wandering
about Europe without any address—"

"His mum will need him, anyhow."

"We'll sort something out." Andy did not
sound as cheerfully confident as usual. She could
tell that he was badly shaken by this blow to their
own plans.

Altogether it had not been a very bright start to
the day. Discussion must wait. There were jobs to
be done before the house opened to the public.

Karen's own thoughts were racing desperately.
Alone in the entrance hall, setting out the
guidebooks and postcards, rolls of tickets and cash-
box, she considered the implications of this news.

Only two weeks before they left. Not much
time to find somebody else. Their other friends
would be committed to their own plans, scattered
all over the place. Just anybody wouldn't do. It
must be somebody who'd fit in.

It was important to go as a foursome. She was sorry Chris couldn't come, and very sorry for the sad reason that prevented him – she liked him, but they weren't close, not as Andy and her cousin were close. Chris had been coming as Andy's friend. If Andy could think of some one else, that would be all right with her. But could he?

Probably. Andy usually found a solution. He was really keen on Julie. This month together in Europe was crucial. They had to sort out their relationship. Find out if they felt it was something long term. The last thing Karen wanted was to get in their way.

Over a quick cup of coffee before opening the doors he said abruptly, "We shall go, of course. Even if we can't find a fourth."

"You and Julie must, that's for sure."

"You too. Why ever not?"

"Because a foursome would work. A threesome wouldn't."

"Oh, rubbish!"

"I'd *be* the rubbish. Feel like it, anyway."

"Oh, *Karen*!"

"I'm sorry," she said firmly.

"I don't think Julie would come if you didn't!"

She had a nasty feeling that he was right. She thought of Julie's parents in Australia. Julie had had enough trouble getting them to agree to this year in London. If she told them now that she was going round Europe with a boyfriend, entirely on their own, they'd hit the roof.

Oh, dear, thought Karen miserably. She didn't

want to wreck the whole scheme, but the idea of trailing round for a month as permanent gooseberry was unspeakable. It would ruin the holiday, maybe ruin some friendships too.

She had looked forward to this trip so much, working and saving to meet the cost. To see the famous places, the pictures and statues she had to learn about, but knew only from book-illustrations and television . . . And, of course, to have *fun* as well. She needed it, after a year of essays and lectures and exam papers.

"We'll have to argue later," said Andy gruffly. He slid back the bolts and people started to file in.

In the lunch-hour they got no nearer to a solution. I suppose it's just as much up to *me*, she thought, to find a fourth. But who? Ideally it should be a man. She couldn't see Andy going round with three girls. But she had no steady boyfriend, no convenient brother. She couldn't ask just anyone.

Two-fifteen. Andy took the first party upstairs. She bent over the cash-box, checking the money against the tickets she had issued.

"Good afternoon . . ." The low, shy greeting startled her. She had not seen the young American walk in.

Had he brought a message from his grandfather, some fresh detail remembered? It seemed rather pointless now, after Sir Peter had demolished their theory.

He was holding out the admission money. "I . . . I thought I'd like to go round again. We never finished the tour yesterday. And as my grand-mother's lying down with a headache . . ."

You saw your chance to slip off the lead, she said to herself. She managed to twist her grin into a friendly smile. It seemed to cheer him up no end.

"Andy's taking a party round. You can catch up with them." He did not look too keen on this. She pushed away the coins he offered. "You mustn't pay again. You didn't get your money's worth yesterday. My silly fault, blowing that whistle."

"You were absolutely justified," he said solemnly. He hovered. "I guess I'd better go up then and join . . . er . . . Andy?"

"Just a moment. May I ask you something?"

"Sure."

"What was your grandfather's regiment in the American army?"

"He was never *in* the American army."

She was startled. Had that kindly old gentle-man been a complete impostor? "But surely," she stammered, "he *is* American?"

"Yeh. But remember, we weren't in the war till 1941. Lots of folk weren't happy about being neutral. Thought we should be in the fight from the word go. Only thing they could do was enlist with the Allies. Simplest way was to slip across the border into Canada. That's what Grandfather did. He was quite a wild young character – you wouldn't think it, now! Only sixteen, but big for his age. They weren't fussy about his birth certificate."

"So . . ." Karen did not know why she was so delighted – any thought of a treasure-hunt had faded by now – but delighted she was. Mr Vandyke was not a liar. Her faith in human nature was restored. "So, he was with the Canadians?"

"1st Canadian Division. With your Eighth Army."

It fitted. She remembered the map in the book. Andy would be thrilled to know that the story still held true. Andy would get to Cosenza, somehow, even if she did not.

People came up to buy postcards. Max lingered awkwardly, then reluctantly trailed off upstairs. There were crowds of visitors that afternoon. She did not see him again.

After closing time she looked round for Andy, but he was full of his own good news.

"Guess what! I've got a replacement for Chris."

"Already? Who?"

"You'll never guess. 'Maxie boy'."

"Max Vandyke? *Never!*"

"If *you* agree. And the old folks." Andy swept on, swamping her with his eagerness. "Sorry to rush things – asking him before I'd checked with you. But it was now or never. And you did say, if I could find someone, it would be OK with you."

"Ye-es. But – *Max*." She almost wailed.

"Max is all right. Did you see his face last night, when we were talking about the trip? Green with envy. Eyes bulging with hopeless yearning. Didn't you notice?"

"How could I? We were sitting side by side."

"Well, you should have seen him light up when

38

I asked him. He'd been asking lots of intelligent questions as we went round – on his own, he's another person. Real sense of humour too."

"You could have fooled *me*. He dared to say yes?"

"Jumped at the chance. The old folks have to go back about then. He could change his flight. No problems about cash, apparently."

"I can believe that," she said acidly.

"He's sure he can fix the old man. He believes in young men being independent. He was a bit of a lad himself, I gather."

She seized the chance to tell him about Mr Vandyke's runaway enlistment in the Canadian army. Andy's enthusiasm redoubled when he realized that the Cosenza incident could well have happened. She thought she had better curb his optimism. "You won't find Mrs V quite so easy," she warned him.

"We'll soon know. They move on tomorrow. I'm going down tonight to discuss things."

"I don't think I'll go, if you don't mind."

"I was going to suggest you didn't, actually."

She hadn't wanted to go, but she was nettled all the same. "Scared I should botch things up?"

"Course not! But another glimpse of your glamour might set alarm bells ringing—"

Karen snorted incredulously.

Andy went on, "She probably imagines you're my girlfriend. Best let her go on thinking so, then she won't be scared you'll get your talons into her precious 'Maxie boy'."

"Idiot!"

"You keep a low profile for the moment, I'll handle this alone. But I can tell Max it's all OK, can't I? I've fixed *you*?"

"Oh, you fix everybody," she said with a grudging laugh.

When he tapped on her door at bedtime he was able to report in triumph that he had.

# FOUR

In Paris, for a few anxious minutes, they feared that Max had let them down. They scanned the milling throng at the station but saw no one in the least like him.

"He's just late," said Julie. She was always so relaxed. Perhaps, Karen thought, it came of being Australian. All that space and sunshine.

"Max wouldn't be late. Not Max. He's probably got lost. All alone in Paris, now Granny's gone home!"

Her cousin laughed. "You *have* got it in for him, haven't you?"

"It's all right," said Andy. "I can see him."

Karen stared unbelievingly at the advancing figure. She had been looking for Max as she remembered him: in a suit, silk tie, crisp white shirt. Now, though his short hair had still to grow, he had conscientiously transformed himself. He was dressed for his new role of vagabond student – jeans, denim jacket, T-shirt, trainers, the lot. Only – everything was *so* new, so spotless and unfaded, without a tatter or split, so *expensive*-looking!

"Oh, *no*." She let out an incredulous groan. "This is too much. He's got a porter. I ask you!"

The little porter dangled the bulging rucksack as if it weighed no more than a party balloon.

The American saw them and waved. He paid

off the porter, heaved the pack on to his back, and hurried towards them.

Karen introduced him to her cousin. "Is your rucksack *so* heavy?" she asked.

"Oh, no, I've only brought what Andy suggested. I hired that guy to make sure that I'd find the right train. My French isn't so good, and this public address system—"

"Utterly incomprehensible," said Julie.

"I don't often use trains," he admitted.

Do you ever, Karen wondered? She could imagine that at home the Vandykes always flew, or zoomed down the state highways in enormous limousines.

A metallic voice began to boom. "Milan!" said Julie. "That's us."

"Better get in and find our places," said Andy.

It was not until late evening that the girls were able to compare notes in whispers as they made ready to doss down in the upper bunks. The young men had tactfully withdrawn into the corridor.

"What do you think of him?" asked Karen anxiously.

"He'll be OK. I rather like him."

"*You* like everybody."

"It's the best way to start."

"I admit, he's better away from his grandmother."

Julie chuckled. "You should have brought her. Sounds quite a character."

There was nothing like an overnight train journey to break the ice. By sunrise, as they stood in line down the corridor, towels and sponge-bags in hand, they all felt more at ease.

Max had had some misgivings during the small hours. He was happier now.

He liked the Australian cousin. Julie was fun. Interesting too, full of stories and experiences. He envied her independence.

She had been temping in London for the past six months, filling temporary jobs while someone was sick or away on vacation. He couldn't imagine "temps" in his grandfather's office. All the secretaries there were dedicated worshippers of their boss. Some had literally grown grey in his service.

Julie had been working for a music publisher, a crazy surgeon in Harley Street, and a bunch of young lawyers in a place called, oddly, the Temple. "They certainly relaxed," she'd recall with her gurgling laugh, "when they got out of court and took their wigs off!" She had hilarious stories about her various employers.

The best thing of all about Julie (thought Max) was that she was Andy's girlfriend. That had been obvious from the first hour. Julie, not Karen, as he'd previously assumed. It might make no difference in the long run. But – it was good to know.

They'd come through the Alps by now. They stopped off at Milan, thankful to quit the train after the long journey. Max felt scruffier than he'd ever felt in his life. He longed for a shower. His grandparents, of course, would have marched straight into the most expensive hotel in sight. He daren't even mention the idea. His friends had to do this trip on the cheap. They'd be extra careful with their money for these first few days.

At least they looked as scruffy as he did, and didn't seem to mind. All the other young people on the train had looked the same. He was beginning to feel part of the general scene. Crumpled clothes, a smear of grease on his sleeve, a roughness already on his unshaven chin . . . He had dreaded being conspicuous. Now, if he watched his step – above all, if he remembered not to flash his money around – he'd get by.

They had coffee, too expensively, on the vast square facing the enormous cathedral. Then Karen wanted to go to the art gallery. Andy and Julie rebelled. They just wanted to sit around in the sun, watching the pigeons and the people going by.

"OK," said Karen. "I don't mind going by myself. I can't go through Milan and not see the pictures."

"I'll come with you," said Max as casually as he could.

She looked at him suspiciously. "Not if pictures bore you."

"They don't." Often they had, when his grandmother had dragged him round galleries at home, telling him what to admire.

"Well . . ." Karen hesitated.

"Must have an escort," said Andy. "Thieves will whizz up behind you on motorbikes and snatch your handbag—"

"I haven't got a handbag."

"Then cheeky young men will pinch your bottom—"

Max said quickly: "*I* want to see this gallery. Let's go together."

"OK." She smiled.

The gallery visit was a success. She knew more about art than he did, more (he guessed) than his grandmother did, but she was not so hot on the wide historical background. He could help there, filling in gaps.

"You know an awful lot of history, Max! I thought your line was Law – and Accountancy?"

"That's the idea. At least, the family's idea."

"But not yours?"

He avoided a plain "no". "There's not much money in history," he said regretfully.

"Oh, *money*!"

He changed the subject hurriedly. "What was it got you on to art? Did it run in the family?"

"You might say so." Her laugh was wry. "*My* grandmother painted flowers on cups and saucers in a pottery."

She told him of her upbringing in Stoke-on-Trent, a big industrial city he'd never heard of, which was apparently famous for its china. Both sides of her family had worked in the trade for generations. He loved the pride with which she spoke of her mother's mother, "the artistic one", whom the head designer had picked out from all the girls in the workshop. If she could have gone to art school she might have really got somewhere.

"But they were just an ordinary working-class family. There wasn't the money for such things."

He teased her gently. "Now *you're* talking about money."

"You can't avoid the subject – entirely."

Next day they went to Rome. They all loved Rome. There was so much to see, though the noise was terrible and crossing the street was almost suicidal. They saw the painted ceiling of the Sistine Chapel, they clambered about the Colosseum, they went round the Villa This and the Villa That until their heads spun and their feet were killing them. "But I daren't go home and say I missed it out," Julie lamented.

From the lofty ramparts of the Castel Sant' Angelo, they looked out over the city and tried to imagine what it had been like in 410 when the Goths burst in.

"Not this size then, I guess," Max said. "But big enough."

It had been, after all, the capital of the Empire, the centre of the known world. For centuries it had been amassing the wealth of conquered countries from Arabia to the Atlantic. It had fallen before Alaric like a house of cards.

"Just imagine the loot," said Andy.

"He didn't enjoy it for long," Karen reminded them.

They hadn't talked much more about their planned visit to Cosenza. They were shy of expecting too much. It was such a slender, far-fetched chance. How could they hope to find a treasure which no one else had, throughout so many centuries?

They would make just a brief stop-over, so that they could say they had been. There was some magnificent scenery anyhow, Andy assured them, the Sila plateau that was only just being opened up to tourists as a national park. That would make a welcome change from the crowded cities.

They took the train on to Naples and saw the buried remains of Pompeii. Andy, as a geologist, felt he must see his first volcano, so they all climbed to the crater of Vesuvius.

After noisy Naples a quiet day or two round Cosenza seemed a good idea. They took another train, one that ran all the way down to Reggio along the coast. Long before it got there Andy looked out of the window and said, "Paola! This is where we change."

They heaved out their baggage and stepped down into Calabria.

# FIVE

Thank goodness, thought Karen, clambering up into the local train, they were off the beaten track at last, no longer surrounded by foreign tourists like themselves. Here, as they rattled inland between the hills, they were really among the Italians.

She wished she could talk to them. This old, old man opposite, for instance, his brown face lined like corrugated cardboard. He'd probably never travelled more than fifty miles from his birthplace.

She was wrong there. He leant across and addressed Andy. "Americano, yes?"

"Er . . . no. *He* is." Andy pointed to Max in the corner. The faded eyes switched over.

"I was in America! Four years." The man held up his tobacco-stained fingers. "Good country!"

"Sure," said Max.

"I was big fool to come back. Here there is nothing." He waved contemptuously at the view.

Karen thought it was a marvellous view. Savage, craggy, bony country. But no doubt the peasants saw it only as a rough, arid land, hard to work, unrewarding. They must be poor.

The old man cleared his throat to spit scornfully, but restrained himself. "We say, if God made this country, He forgot afterwards. No one does anything. For us, nothing!"

A fleshy young man in a dark suit had been listening. Now he joined in.

"Excuse, please. You must not pay attention to this silly old man. He knows nothing. It is this ignorance we have to deal with. Always the South has been backward. We do all we can. We build dams to irrigate and make electricity, we undertake public works for the unemployed, we encourage tourists. The government—"

"The government!" cackled the old man. "*You* speak as if you were the government. Because you have this." He tapped the black briefcase which the young man held on his lap. "You are no-account, you. If you were somebody you would sit in the first class! Or drive in your fine automobile." This time he spat.

The young man clutched at his dignity. He smirked apologetically at the girls. "I will not argue with this ill-mannered old fool. We must not spoil your pleasure in this picturesque landscape. I trust you will pass a good stay in Calabria." He snapped open his briefcase and began to sort his papers importantly.

"Interesting," Karen murmured softly.

She could understand the despair of the poor – she knew that they emigrated in thousands to seek a better livelihood abroad, and sometimes made a mistake in coming back. It might well be, as the young man said, that the government was bringing in schemes to improve matters. But, as she'd learned in her own country, government schemes didn't always come up to expectation and people had a very suspicious attitude towards officials.

It was only about sixty kilometres to Cosenza but the journey, climbing up from sea-level, took an hour and a half. The town, at first sight, was not impressive. The guide-book had been blunt about that. *Cosenza can be skipped, as it lacks interest. But it is a good centre for more interesting places nearby.* In fact, a convenient starting point in their quest for Mr Vandyke's bomb-crater.

Before they left the station Andy said, "We must ask the way to the youth hostel." The girls instantly rebelled. They had used inexpensive hostels in all the cities. Julie said firmly that for one night at least she wanted the luxury of her own bathroom. Karen supported her. Max, she noticed, looked thankful when Andy meekly gave way.

It was not far to the modern centre of the little city. They looked at the two or three hotels, had a quick conference on the pavement, chose one that did not look alarmingly costly, and trooped in. A drowsy young man roused himself behind the reception desk. His expression was not conspicuously welcoming. Karen would have called it supercilious.

Yes, they had two double rooms available. "With bath?" Julie demanded. "But of course!" He looked pained. He offered the registration forms for signature. "And the number of your car, signore?" he asked Andy.

"No car."

"No car, signore?" The eyebrows rose in disapproval.

He knows damn well we haven't a car, thought

50

Karen angrily. He summed us up at sight. He thinks we're lowering the tone of the establishment. She wished they'd gone to the hostel.

A porter gathered up their rucksacks. Max turned to the receptionist. "Say, I can call New York from here?"

"Certainly, signore." The man became more respectful. Good old Max, she thought, as they filed into the lift.

Upstairs she felt more certain that they had done the right thing. Their budget could stand one night of civilized comfort. While Julie soaked luxuriously, the fragrance of free bath salts stealing from the alcove to pervade the whole room, Karen scribbled an overdue news bulletin to her parents. The hotel's impressive note-heading would reassure them that their daughter was safe and respectably accommodated.

When they had all freshened up they set forth to find a café and explore while the daylight lasted. The old quarter lay just across the river, climbing the lower slopes of a steep green hill crowned by the long pale walls and corner towers of the medieval Castello.

They paused on the bridge to peer down at the river, shallow at this late stage of the summer. Andy opened the local town-plan he had picked up at the desk. "This must be the Busento."

"Where this bloke Alaric . . ." began Julie.

"Yes, where this bloke Alaric . . ."

"It doesn't look much."

"Gibbon called it 'a small river that washes the walls of Consentia'," said Max.

"They can still do with a wash." Julie looked round. "I thought you said he had a secret funeral? Looks sort of public hereabouts."

"I told you," said Andy patiently, "we've considered all that. It must have been some way from the town." Their whole theory, linking Alaric's grave with the spoon in the bomb-crater, depended on the site being some miles distant from the city.

"Then why did this Edward Gibbon say—"

"He didn't *say* the burial itself was overlooked from the walls," Max explained. "Anyhow, I guess he never came to Cosenza himself. Never travelled much south of Naples. Folks didn't in the eighteenth century. He just read all the old records and books he could lay hands on, then wrote up the story in elegant prose, using his own imagination."

Julie seized on the word. "Then the treasure may be all imagination?"

Karen often wondered herself. But she said, "Modern experts seem to accept the story. But nothing's ever been found."

They walked on into the old quarter, past ancient churches and one-time noble mansions. As they went they argued about tomorrow's programme. Where should they make a start?

Gibbon had written of "a secret spot". And why massacre all the unfortunates who had done the digging if the treasure had been buried in full view of the city walls?

They trudged up the winding track to the castle and flung themselves on the grass. The view up here was splendid. The mountains seemed to encircle Cosenza on every side. The massive plateau of the Sila dominated the view. Andy thought he could identify the main summit, Botte Donato. "Nearly two thousand metres."

"Around six thousand feet," said Max.

Below them spread the rooftops of the city. They could trace the course of the rivers, checking against the blue lines on the town-plan. The Busento joined a larger river, the Crati, just below the bridge they had crossed. But upstream it had tributaries of its own. Suppose the Goths had chosen one of these to dam? Would Gibbon, writing his book far away in Switzerland, ever have known?

"I guess we're approaching this from the wrong angle," said Max. "The vital clue can't be in Gibbon, or someone would have followed it up and found the treasure ages ago. The clue is in Grandfather's bomb-crater and what he reckons he saw in the soil around him. No one else has ever had that clue. It's the crater we've got to trace."

Andy triumphantly played his trump card. "*This* should help." He pulled out a shabby-looking old map and unfolded it. "My uncle dug this out for me – no, not literally 'dug' – it had been kept with all *my* grandfather's wartime stuff. Remember, he was with the Eighth Army, like yours, Max. Only he *had* a map – he was a major by then – and this is the sheet for Cosenza."

"This is something," said Max, almost excitedly.

"Forget about Alaric and Gibbon and all that

lot," Andy instructed them. "See here. You're a general advancing on the town from the south. You think the bridges are most likely mined. In case they are, you detach troops to make river-crossings and outflank any Germans who may be still around. Where are the likely places? Remember, we're looking for a valley with steep sides – that means the contours will run close together – and there's got to be a village, and a church . . ."

They all scrutinized the map eagerly. Though none of the others had Andy's fluency in map-reading it took only a few minutes for them to accept his verdict: there were just three spots which fulfilled all the conditions. One or other must have been the scene of Mr Vandyke's experience.

"So this is where we start looking tomorrow," said Max.

"And if it isn't the scene of Alaric's funeral as well?" said the sceptical Julie.

"We'll have to blame my grandfather for imagining he saw things when he didn't."

They walked back to the hotel in the glow of the sunset. Max said, "Guess I'll call my mother before we go in to dinner. It'll be around midday, back home." Going up in the lift they arranged to meet again in the foyer in half an hour.

Karen was first to come down again. She sat in a corner, quietly studying the other guests – some new arrivals signing in with mounds of impressive baggage, a German family filing into the bar, an anxious young man waiting for his girlfriend to reappear from the lift.

The first time that the lift-doors opened, how-ever, it was for Max. She raised her hand in salute, but he was distracted by the receptionist. The man was showing him something in a glossy magazine. He sounded effusive, pleased with himself.

She had never seen Max look so cross. "Give it me," he said curtly.

"But, signore—"

"Give it me, please."

Max pulled out his wallet, laid a note on the desk.

"But of course, signore—"

"Thank you," said Max between his teeth.

He turned and took a few steps. She heard the paper rip once, twice, three times, as he tore the pages across, then the thud as they dropped into a bin.

Max had not seen her. At that moment Andy and Julie stepped out of the lift. He spun round to greet them. She was able to stand up, unob-trusively, and move over to join them. Max would not know that she had witnessed anything.

The mystery nagged at the back of her mind throughout the meal. She itched to ask Max about it, but decided better not. Not until they had all gone up to bed did she find a chance to do anything.

She picked up the letter to her parents. "I'll just have to go down again," she told Julie. "I can get a stamp at the desk. The box may be cleared first thing in the morning."

The receptionist had gone off duty. The night

porter sold her a stamp. She drifted casually across the foyer, studying the show cases of local pottery and textiles. Good! The wastepaper bin had not been emptied. She stooped quickly, gathered the jagged scraps of glossy magazine.

Better examine them alone. She felt guilty. Julie would say – truthfully – that she was being nosy.

So in the late-night solitude of the Ladies, she fitted the torn pieces together like jigsaw puzzles. It did not take long to assemble the page she was looking for.

Suddenly the face of Mr Vandyke was smiling at her. And, on the scrap adjoining, was Max himself. They seemed to be in a boat. A typical illustration from a gossip column in some snob magazine. It did not take much knowledge of Italian to understand the caption.

*Il multimilionario americano, Paul Vandyke . . .*

She got the general drift of the remainder. Relaxing on the lake of his estate in Virginia . . . accompanied by one of his five grandsons, Max . . .

She had guessed that the Vandykes were rich – but not *that* rich. Her mind reeled. Multimillionaire!

Her first thought was, how exciting, what a thing to tell Julie. Then she thought again. Max didn't want them to know. He'd be hopelessly embarrassed. He wanted so much to be treated just as one of the gang. He'd clearly been furious with the creepy little man at the desk.

She must not breathe a word to anyone. She tore the glossy pieces into even smaller scraps, dropped them back in the bin, and stepped into the lift.

Julie was already half asleep. "Mailed your letter all right? G'night. Sleep tight."

Tired though she was, Karen could not do so for some time.

# SIX

"Now let's get the hell out of here," said Max with unusual violence when they had paid their bills.

He had not meant to let his irritation show, but that obsequious guy behind the desk reminded him of last night's episode over the photograph. Expecting him to be pleased! *Pleased* – when for him the whole charm of this trip was to escape from the privileged world he normally lived in, and be treated like anyone else in his age-group.

Outside on the pavement Julie said, having misunderstood his tone, "Yes, the bills *were* a bit stiff, weren't they? The little extras they stuck on, and then these local taxes and percentages—"

"I'm not worried about the bill. I . . . I just want to get moving, that's all."

They were all eager now to head for the open country and put their theories to the test. Julie insisted, however, that they should visit the market stalls and lay in some emergency food-supplies.

"If we're going out into the bush, so to speak—"

"This is Italy," Andy said impatiently, "not your Australian outback. The map shows *villages*."

"Fine. But it does no harm to be independent."

The hotel bills were still very much on Julie's conscience. That yearning yesterday, for a night in a hotel with bathroom *en suite* . . . She blamed herself for involving them all in extra expense. "In this weather we can just doss down in the open for a night or two. Fun. Save thousands of lire!"

So they bought long crusty rolls, cheese, slices of ham, tomatoes, a melon, a bottle of red wine, another of mineral water . . . Andy had packed water-purification tablets so that they could use streams in emergencies.

Karen was much attracted by a regional speciality – a luscious-looking, heart-shaped cake, its pink icing decorated by a necklace of sugar pearls. Max was sorely tempted to buy it for her, but with all this talk of economy in the air his courage failed him. Probably it would not have travelled well in a rucksack.

Andy consulted the army map again, checking it against the street-plan to make sure that they were leaving the city in the right direction, and said: "Here we go, then."

Soon, as the buildings thinned out and at last fell behind them, they could see the high plateau rearing up on the skyline.

"There's one thing," said Andy, "if we don't find anything in the end – and most likely we shan't – we're not wasting our time. This'll take us straight on into the Sila." In the Sila, the guide-book promised, were untamed mountain areas, with "rolling woods, enfolding great jade green lakes". They might see wolves and wild boar.

Max had a suspicion that Andy was feeling a sudden chill of doubt. All along, he had been the keen one, his optimism upholding them all. But now the crunch was near. By tomorrow they might be facing the fact that they could not identify the scene of his grandfather's adventure and that, quite literally, they hadn't a clue. Max felt a great sympathy for Andy – almost a guilt that *his*, Max's, grandfather had innocently led Andy into such an embarrassing fiasco. Andy, going on now about the scenery of the Sila, sounded as though he were preparing them all for disappointment, planning where they could go next to blot out their sense of failure.

They could see the river again now – if it was *the* river – far below their road, its course strewn with white boulders. Peasants moved to and fro on the slopes. Black donkeys browsed here and there amid the scrub.

The valley narrowed after a while. At a bend in the road they saw that it was walled off by a high barrier, a smooth curving cliff of sheer white concrete. They stopped in their tracks.

Andy said: "Must be one of the new dams the man in the train was talking about."

"If there's a lake the other side of that . . ." Karen's voice tailed off in dismay.

The same thought had occurred to Max. The valley beyond that immense wall might be buried beneath millions of gallons of water. The spot where Grandfather had crouched might now be a hundred feet below the surface. Their quest would have finished before it had begun.

"Well, let's know the worst," said Andy.

A service road, doubtless made for the construction of the dam, forked off from the highway, slanting across the scrubby mountainside. It brought them after a few minutes to a point from which they had a view of the valley beyond.

"It's OK," Karen gasped. "Still empty!"

The upper valley was browner, more rugged, stark and rather grim. Its floor was green, however, and the river still gleamed in patches between the tumbled rocks.

"There's a bloke waving," said Julie.

From a building at the near end of the dam a figure had emerged. He cupped his hands and shouted. His voice echoed across the emptiness, resonant but unintelligible.

"He's not just saying good-morning," said Karen. "We'd better stop. He's got a gun."

The man came striding up to meet them. Another man appeared and followed after him. He too carried a shotgun.

The first man was gesturing with his free hand, emphatic sweeps horizontally across his body. "*Vietato, signori! Vietato!*"

That was one word they all understood. They had seen it on warning notices. "What's 'forbidden'?" Andy muttered rebelliously. The man had a peaked uniform cap. Probably a watchman or something. He was talking non-stop as he drew near.

"I wish I knew Italian," Karen sounded troubled.

"Sometimes," said Max, "it's better *not* to understand what they say."

He stepped forward, putting on his most harmless smile. "American tourist," he called out amiably. Those words were usually well received.

They were now. The man smiled, turned and called to the colleague overtaking him, "*Turista! Turista americano!*"

The second man had a more discouraging

expression. He kept on repeating "*vietato*" and asking incomprehensible questions, presumably demanding to know where they were going and what was their business.

By now they were all gathered together in a little group. Max realized that, unintentionally, he seemed to have become the spokesman. He must do his best to convince these men that he and his friends were only harmless sightseers. "*Bella vista*," he said admiringly, waving vaguely at the encircling scenery, which certainly was rather beautiful, if in a somewhat savage way.

"*Si, si, bella vista*," agreed the first man without undue enthusiasm.

Max noticed that Julie, who seemed knowledgeable about wild flowers and plants, had plucked some dazzling paper-thin rock roses and sprigs of myrtle. He pointed to these, hoping that, as a sign of interest in botany, they might convince the Italians of their innocent intentions.

The two men did not look impressed. The second one enquired hopefully, "*Sigaretta americana?*"

Max shook his head apologetically. That would have sweetened the atmosphere considerably, but no one in the party smoked. The Italian looked disappointed and cross. Max slipped him a thousand-lire note. The Italian cheered up noticeably. But when Max moved as if to start walking down the road again the man put out an arm to bar the way.

Andy had been silent too long. Now he broke in, impatiently, "We don't want to go near his precious dam. Does he think we're going to blow it up or something?" He pointed towards the dam, shook his head emphatically. "No." Conveniently the word was very similar in both languages. Then he turned and pointed down the steep hillside towards the river at the bottom, making it clear that this was the way they wanted to go.

The first Italian said, regretfully, "*Non, signore.*"

Andy challenged him. "*Vietato?*"

The watchman hesitated, shrugged his shoulders. "*Vietato, non, signore. Pericoloso.*"

That was another warning word they had all learned from seeing it on electricity pylons and elsewhere. So, thought Max, it isn't actually forbidden to go that way, but it's dangerous. He wondered why.

The two Italians were trying to explain, but none of the friends could make head or tail of what they said. Andy was obstinate. So were the men. At last the first watchman, after a furtive look round, uttered one word in a conspiratorial whisper, as if to clinch the argument.

"*Lupomanari!*"

"*Lupomanari?*" echoed Andy. Both men hissed in a shocked manner. "What's that supposed to mean?"

"*Lupus* is Latin for wolf," Max said.

"They're warning us against wolves?" Andy was incredulous. "At this time of year?" Even the tourist leaflet didn't guarantee a glimpse of wolves in summer time and it assured the most nervous visitor that there was no risk of being attacked.

Finally, to keep the watchmen happy, they gave way and retraced their steps as far as the public highway, and then continued on their way. Soon a twist in the valley took them out of sight of the dam and its guardians. There was then nothing to prevent their striking down a steep little path that would take them to the river.

The air was still. It was an uncannily silent world. When a raven croaked suddenly, its harsh cry, *pruk!*, startled them all. The bird sailed out over the void of air, spreading its black wings, crossing in moments to the opposite mountainside.

"There must have been forests in the old days," said Andy. "They cut them down. The top soil got washed away. And they'd get landslides. They were gradually turning it into a dead valley." Andy was a keen conservationist and got very bitter about such things. Only the floor of the valley was green and showed signs of cultivation, both sides of the winding river.

Max wondered if this *had* been Grandfather's valley. He tried to picture the khaki-clad Canadians threading their way down through the low bushes in single file, ready to flatten themselves on the ground at the first rattle of an enemy machine-gun.

Karen cried out. "Look! The village!"

It was coming into view on the other side of the valley, a jumble of buff walls and terracotta tiles climbing the slope.

"There's the church," said Julie. Its bell-tower was unmistakable, an uplifted finger above the housetops.

"But where's the big cross?" Andy demanded. "Mr Vandyke said it was still higher up the hill." They stared, but no one could pick out a wayside calvary, the vital clue they sought.

No smoke-haze rose from the chimneys, no dog barked, not a voice broke the stillness. "I guess the whole place is deserted," Max said. "They must have moved the folks out. All those houses will be under water when they fill the reservoir."

"Perhaps we've come just in time," said Karen.

"I wish we could see that cross," said Andy. "Even if it got bombed that day, surely they'd have put up another."

As they hurried down towards the river it was obvious that the valley had been abandoned for some months. The vines had not been pruned. Julie remembered the well-tended vineyards in Australia. Here the unpruned growth straggled along weedy terraces. The people had known they would never gather this year's grapes.

On the flat ground at the bottom the little plots were smothered in weeds, almost indistinguishable from the narrow ridges of tussocky grass marking the boundaries.

The river, as Mr Vandyke had described it, was very easy to cross. It was, after all, nearly the same time of year. Often they had only to stride from one flat rock to another or take a flying leap on to the next bed of shingle.

If this really *was* the place, Max thought, it had certainly changed in some respects. Then it must have been thoroughly churned up by the bombs. The peasants had patiently filled in those craters, levelled the ground, and staked out their individual holdings again.

They'd planted trees again – olives, almonds, peaches – and they'd come to maturity over the intervening years. It was pathetic that, with the building of the dam, all that effort would produce no more.

They must now be walking across the very stretch where Grandfather would have been (if this was the village) when the Nazi bombers dived from the sky. He raised his eyes to measure how far it was to the first houses, where the little girls had waved.

He saw something that brought a shout of triumph to his lips.

Now that they were getting close under the mountainside, its upper heights had vanished from view. The church came into silhouette against the sky. At this steep angle only one higher point was visible.

"There's the cross!" he cried.

Previously it must have been merged into the general background. Now, just above the church roof, a little to the left, its tip stood up, its shape unmistakable, the landmark they were looking for.

# SEVEN

The alignment of church and cross fitted neatly into Mr Vandyke's recollections. It seemed almost too good to be true. But not incredible. They had the old army map in all its details. To Andy's practised eye it showed the only possible places along the river that would match the information they had.

"It's not even a case of 'first time lucky'," he insisted, all his old confidence flooding back. "We started on this place because it's the first you come to as you follow up the river. And for the same reason the troops were sent here to make the crossing – it was the nearest point to the town they were trying to outflank."

"What do we do now?" asked Karen.

"Eat!"

No one argued against that. The deserted village was rather a disappointment – coffee would have been welcome if obtainable – but in other respects the solitude would be an asset. No one would appear to stare and question, to challenge their right to poke about in this derelict ground at will.

They found shade under some cypresses. Cicadas whirred in the bleached grass. Amusing lizards flicked about over the rocks. Max earned a cheer for himself when he produced a thermos flask, which he had quietly tipped the waiter to fill with coffee after breakfast.

"Have you any more surprises?" Julie demanded. "No wonder your pack weighs a ton!"

"The clerk in the store suggested it, when I was buying my kit in Paris. I guessed he'd know best what I needed."

Karen smiled to herself. No doubt the shop assistant had sized up Max as a naive young man to whom money was no object. If he'd recommended an ice-axe or a climbing rope Max would have probably fallen for the sales talk. No, she checked herself sharply. I'm being unfair. Max is not a fool.

The coffee was more than welcome. Only Julie sternly insisted that they kept some in the flask. They did not know when they would have a chance to refill it. And if they were going to camp out tonight . . .

There was general agreement that they should. No sense in leaving this place until they had looked round properly. They had plenty of food. They had better reconnoitre the village, make sure that there really was nobody about, and find somewhere to spend the night.

"Establish our base," said Julie firmly. "Then it'll be time enough to start thinking about old Alaric and his gold." She surveyed the scene with a sceptical eye. "Going to be a real needle in a haystack job if you ask me."

Andy and Max discussed the problem in practical terms as they walked across the flat ground to where the village began to climb the slope.

"If it was a properly organized dig," said Andy

wistfully, "with dozens of volunteers, proper equipment, all the time in the world—"

"None of which we have!"

"Exactly. We can only hope that my hunch will work out and provide a lead – a short cut."

Andy clung to his theory that the river had changed course since the Goths had dammed it and buried their king with the plunder of Rome. Mr Vandyke had seen things peeping out of the loose soil in his bomb-crater. And Mr Vandyke had already crossed the river – the river where it ran today.

"So we've got to find the *old* watercourse."

"But how?" asked Max. "After centuries of digging and ploughing – not to mention bombing and—"

"It's amazing how things show. We can trace prehistoric fields in England that you'd never suspect even when you were walking across them. Aerial photographs will show up the whole pattern—"

"Too bad we haven't an aeroplane," said Julie.

"Perhaps," Karen suggested gently, "when we get right up to that cross, and look straight down on to the bottom of the valley, we *might* get that sort of effect."

"It's worth trying anyhow," said Andy. He sounded grateful for her support.

They reached the first forlorn houses. Some windows were carefully shuttered. Others, their glass removed, were dark eyeless sockets. Doors gaped open to reveal the emptiness within. Karen felt a pang for all the departed families to whom this place had once been home.

The steep lane forked at a public fountain. Clear water still jetted from the mouth of a dolphin, splashing into a trough below. Here the women and girls would have met to fill their pails and gossip. Here mules would have paused to drink.

A poster was stuck on the wall. The four friends pieced out its meaning with what scraps of Italian they knew. It was an official proclamation.

All inhabitants must evacuate the village with their livestock and possessions. The final date was menacing in its bold black type. *APRILE 30.*

"Three months ago!" cried Karen in disgust. "Just like a government! They turn out all these poor people – and still, after three months, they haven't even *started* to flood the valley."

Close by was a schoolhouse, set back in its tiny triangle of yard. The door stood ajar. They filed in.

It was cool and light, the white walls cobwebbed but otherwise clean. Withered leaves had drifted into corners. The miniature desks and benches stood neatly in their rows, old, ink-stained, knife-scarred, not worth removing to another school.

Drawings and paintings, pinned on a board, made a ghostly rustle in the draught from the door. But they brought this dead place to life again, recalling the personalities of the vanished pupils. There were houses, the children's own homes no doubt, and the church up the hill.

Someone had drawn a mounted policeman, a dashing Carabiniere, patrolling the mountains on his splendid steed. There was a long-eared donkey, a black cat with brilliant lemon-yellow eyes, a caricature of a furious old woman chasing a boy with her stick. There had been a caption under this last picture, but it had been scribbled over in blue pencil. Karen could just decipher the name *Donna Margherita.*

She laughed. "Censored by Teacher! But too good to tear up."

Andy came over. "We might do worse than doss down in here. It's clean. It doesn't smell, or anything. And – well, it *was* a public building, sort of. It's not like barging into what was somebody's home."

They all saw his point. The schoolhouse was spartan but wholesome enough. They explored its facilities. "Basic," said Julie frankly. Probably no worse, thought Karen, than many a little country school at home had managed with until a generation or two ago. No running water. For washing, the little boys and girls must have filled their plastic bowls from the fountain outside. The bowls were still there and would be handy, small though they were – better than taking turns to wash at the spurting jet from the dolphin's mouth. The small scale of the other arrangements provoked some mildly indelicate mirth.

"It'll do us fine for a night or two," said Julie as they crossed the playground.

They were tempted to dump their rucksacks there and then, before completing their climb to the top of the village. Caution held them back. The place was empty except for the droning insects, the silent scampering lizards. There was no human voice, no challenging bark of dog, no lingering memory of woodsmoke or cooking oil on the hotly quivering air of the afternoon. The very mule-droppings had long ago powdered and merged with the dust of the road. Of *course* the place was empty – "empty as a beer-can," said Julie – yet even she was strangely reluctant to be parted from her rucksack until they had made sure.

So, grumbling a little at their own timidity, they shouldered their burdens again and set their faces to the hill.

Gradually, passing one derelict dwelling after another, they gathered confidence. They poked their heads into doorways, then without hesitation peered around them. They were invading nobody's privacy. These abandoned buildings were as remote and impersonal as the ruins of Pompeii. Andy pounced on an old spade. "Might come in handy," he said, and propped it against the wall outside to be collected on their way back. Further on, they found a fork with a broken handle, a shovel, a trowel, a dented bucket, a pickaxe that would be invaluable for breaking up the hard-baked earth.

In an outbuilding close by was an equally welcome find: a heap of last year's straw. "We'll have a few armfuls of this when we go down again," said Andy. "That schoolhouse floor will get harder as the night goes on."

"What about rats?" Karen tried not to sound nervous.

"Soon see." Andy fetched the shovel from the other house. "Stand back!" He poked and slapped the straw vigorously, but no living creatures emerged.

Relieved, they continued up the lane and came to the church. "They've taken the bells," said Max, pointing upwards to the tower. The door was closed but not locked. It squealed back on unoiled hinges. The stoup for holy water was long since dry. The interior was bare as a bone. No garish sacred pictures or images lent colour to the plastered walls.

"Nothing in here," said Andy.

"Looter!" said Karen in mock disapproval.

"There might be some bits of candle," said Julie with her usual practical instinct. "Remember, we'll only have our torches tonight."

Karen followed her into the tiny vestry. Good old Julie! On the window-ledge was quite a heap of candle-ends burnt down to various lengths. Apart from the altar there had probably been a statuette of the Virgin or some saint, where villagers had lighted candles to support their prayers.The sacred image had been taken away. There seemed no irreverence in gathering up the candle-ends.

They found Max and Andy standing by another door which led up ladders to the bell-tower.

"Are you going up?" Julie asked.

"No point, I think." That, from Andy, was an

unexpected response. But he and Max seemed more interested in a stack of bags neatly arranged round the foot of the ladder.

"Cement, would you say?" Max was suggesting.

"Too small, I'd have thought," said Andy. Max stooped forward as if to poke one of the bags. Andy stopped him with quite unusual sharpness.

"I wouldn't touch them."

"Sorry."

"Whatever's in them is no business of ours." That again was unlike Andy, usually as inquisitive as any cat. He closed the door with extreme care. Seeing their puzzled expressions he said, as casually as he could: "You never know. There may be a scheme to demolish some of these buildings. Best not touch anything."

"You mean," said Karen wide-eyed, "it could be explosive? That stuff – semtex?"

Andy shrugged. "No idea. The bags look too small for ordinary plaster or cement or anything. It's the *kind* of thing – if we were back home – I'd be inclined to mention to the police. But here – well, there *are* no police, there's no one to report anything to. And anyhow, as I said, it's no business of ours."

"I'm glad we're not sleeping in here," said Julie.

The houses petered out. The road climbed steeply zigzag and suddenly, at a bend, they saw the calvary outlined against a scudding cloud. The cross was all of three metres high, the figure of Christ roughly carved and painted, the scarlet wounds faded by the weather.

"At least they didn't take this away," said Karen.

"Maybe the water won't come up this high," Max said.

Andy mounted the steps and surveyed the valley below.

"How's the photographic eye?" Julie enquired.

He screwed up his eyes against the sun. "Not much good. You *think* you're on to something, a line of bushes, say, that might once have followed a river-bank. Then it peters out. Or there's a bump in the ground, and you know that a stream couldn't ever have run that way—"

"Unless the bump had been made later by a landslide – or an earthquake?" Karen suggested.

That was the trouble. In Calabria, with its history of earthquakes, large and small, not to mention landslides and ordinary winter floods, there was no telling what changes this valley had seen over fifteen centuries.

They went down to the schoolhouse again, picking up the old spade and the other tools they had found. Then, feeling free at last to dump their rucksacks, they returned for armfuls of straw to soften the stone slabs of the classroom. It took several trips to carry enough for comfort.

As an hour of two of daylight remained, Andy was keen to take another look at the ground the soldiers must have been crossing when the Nazi bombers swooped down on them. Max went with him. The girls agreed that they had walked enough that day.

"We'll stay at base," said Julie.

"You . . . you don't mind us leaving you?" Max, as usual, was polite and rather hesitant.

"What is there to be scared of?"

"What indeed?"

Max and Andy went off, carrying the spade and the broken fork. "Just in case," said Andy.

The girls unpacked, spread out their sleeping-bags, filled wash-bowls from the fountain outside, and generally freshened up.

"You know, Andy's really bitten with this treasure bug," said Julie.

Karen laughed. "He loves a challenge."

"What beats me – he's not thinking of the *money*. In fact, he reckons that if we did find anything, we wouldn't be allowed to keep it."

"I think that's right." Karen herself had never built any hopes of fabulous wealth for themselves. Like Andy, she'd been attracted to the mere puzzle of it all. And, with her interest in art history and museums, it was exciting to think that they might – just might – turn up something of importance. "I don't know about Italian law," she went on, "but if it's like most countries nowadays it wouldn't be a question of finders keepers. The government would take over from the moment we reported it. I expect we'd be given some sort of reward. For being honest." And, she added to herself, we'd get some credit.

That *would* be wonderful, though she'd never admit the thought to a living soul. To be one of the people who'd found Alaric's lost treasure! Whatever else she did – whatever career she achieved in her chosen line, even if she finished up as Professor or Doctor or Director – it would still be remembered and whispered: *"When she was still only a first-year student . . ."*

Julie brought her back to earth. "Well, *I'm* not bothered," she said cheerfully. "Wouldn't say no to a reward if we got one, but I didn't come on this trip with any expectations. Just came for the ride."

Fine, thought Karen. I expect it's all any of us will get.

Andy and Max seemed distinctly subdued when they came back in the twilight. They cheered up at sight of the candle-lit supper, set out on the teacher's oblong table, the red wine winking in its bottle.

"There sure is some ground to cover," said Max.

"Any leads?" Karen asked.

Andy said cautiously that there were one or two spots he wanted to look at more closely tomorrow. "But what we really need is a metal-detector."

"Why didn't you bring one?" said Julie.

Andy gave a rather hollow laugh. "Have you ever seen one?"

"Can't say I have."

"Well, it's not something you can slip into your pocket, like a magnet or a compass. It's got a long handle – about a metre long – control-box, search-head, headphones, cable . . . You can't lug all that around with you, just on the off chance."

"I wonder," said Max thoughtfully, "if we could hire one – or buy one – in Cosenza."

"Might be tricky."

"At home," said Karen, "I believe you have to get a licence from the government. I don't know whether there's a lot of red tape here."

"We could enquire." Max sounded unusually firm.

"It's awkward – not one of us can really talk Italian—"

"Money does. Fluently."

A typical Vandyke reaction, she thought, with a hint of her old prejudice. If you want something you can always get it – provided you pay. Life was easy for some.

No more was said. They ate their supper, enjoyed the rough red wine, finished the last precious drops of coffee, now rather tepid even in the flask. Tomorrow . . . They would debate tomorrow when it came.

Karen lifted one of the desk-lids to put away what was left of the bread. Not all the desk had been completely emptied. She saw a ball, a stub of pencil, a sheet of paper. Another picture, which somehow had missed being pinned up in the display.

A pity. Even in the wavering candle-light she could see it had power and character above the average. Perhaps it was by the same child who had drawn the angry old woman. Perhaps by the boy she had been chasing.

This was quite different in subject. Three men on a mountain ridge under a full moon. Only – they did not have human faces. They had animal heads. Dogs? But not at all like cuddly dressed-up dogs in a storybook. There was something sinister about them.

"What on *earth* . . .?" Julie asked. Karen held out the picture. "They've been having a lesson on ancient Egypt," her cousin suggested. "Who was that god with a dog's head?"

"You mean Anubis? The God of the Dead."

Andy peered over Julie's shoulder. "Why three of him?" He took the paper. "I don't think those *are* dogs' heads. More like wolves."

"Does it matter?" said Julie.

"That bloke at the dam, this morning, muttered something about wolves."

"These are really men, though."

"In some of these remote villages they say the peasants still believe in werewolves."

The others laughed, but with a faint unease. "Pardon my ignorance," said Julie, "but just what exactly *are* werewolves? I thought they were just something in horror films."

"It's an old superstition," Andy explained. "They're men who can turn themselves into wolves at night – and then back into men next morning."

"Oh, I know men like that," said Julie disdainfully, "but I wouldn't go out with them."

The discussion ended on that joking note. Karen slipped the drawing away. She could understand why it had not been pinned up. The teacher didn't want the kids frightened. It was too spooky.

They turned in soon afterwards. It had been a strenuous day. Andy nipped out the candles and crawled into his sleeping-bag. Soon they were all asleep.

For Karen, however, it was an uneasy sleep, troubled by gruesome dreams from which she was thankful to wake. She was then disappointed to realize it was not morning. The pallid light, which revealed reassuringly the softly breathing humps of her companions, came not from dawn but from the moonbeams slanting from the high windows. Her watch said twenty past two.

It was good to be awake, to have escaped the weird wolf-headed phantoms of her nightmare, but not so good that she seemed unable to drop off again immediately. Her mother's advice in such cases was to get up, move about for a few minutes, take a drink of water or something.

She slid cautiously out of her sleeping-bag, groped for her trainers, crept to the door and eased it open.

The moon was almost full, riding a cloudless sky. Like the moon in the child's drawing – ugh, no, she didn't want to be reminded of that picture. She walked across the yard, even her own black shadow alarming. Out here, away from her friends, the stillness of the dead village was even more unnerving.

Just then the utter silence was broken. She stopped, froze where she stood.

The sound came from a little distance, not loud but oddly penetrating. Was it a voice? It was wordless. It rose and fell, with silences between. She could not guess what sort of creature produced it.

One thing was certain. The village was not as lifeless as it had seemed by day. Someone, or something, was just up there, beyond the school-yard wall.

She forced herself to raise her eyes. She did not want to see anything, and thank God she did not. But she heard that eerie sound again, a sort of pleading wail.

She felt defenceless, standing there in that brilliant moonlight in her flimsy pyjamas. She raced for the porch, flung herself inside and closed the door. There were no bolts, no key in the lock. The sleepers did not stir. She longed to rouse Andy, get him to help her shove some desks against the door. But what could she *say*? She'd had a nightmare, heard a weird noise outside . . . no, she hadn't actually *seen* anything . . . They would all pull her leg for the rest of the holiday.

Without waking any of them she carried a small bench to the door and placed it so that it would be knocked over by anyone trying to come in. Then she tiptoed swiftly back to her sleeping-bag and snuggled down thankfully inside.

Her troubles were not over. A soft sound over-head caused her to open her eyes again. The nearest window was small, high and unglazed. Its beam of moonlight was now blocked by a dark shape. As she stared up at it, momentarily petrified, that shape somehow uncoiled and launched itself, landing with a faint plop upon her.

Suddenly there was a warm breath upon her cheek, a deep throbbing murmur like a kettle approaching the boil. She thrust out a cautious hand and felt soft fur.

"Puss!" she whispered reprovingly but infinitely relieved. "You devil! You scared the living daylights out of me."

# EIGHT

It was bright morning when Karen woke again. The dream about the cat was instantly vivid in her mind. But it had been no dream. The cat was beside here, jet black, narrowed eyes like slivers of lemon peel, grooming itself fastidiously.

Julie cried out. "Whatya know! Where did *you* come from?" She sat up, entranced.

Andy groaned in his sleeping-bag, struggling back to consciousness. "Black cat? Should be lucky!"

"Must have stayed behind when the folks quit," said Max.

"But what's he been living on?" Karen demanded, caressing the plump warm body. This was no half-starved stray. "If he'd been living rough for three months he'd be a wildcat by now."

"Dead more likely." Andy came over, stroked the furry back. The cat accepted his attentions graciously. "There must still be someone living not far away."

"That reminds me," Karen began. But before she could tell them of last night's incident she heard the strange wordless call again.

The cat heard it too and streaked for the door, still barricaded by the bench. Someone was struggling to push it back. "Nero!" a high-pitched woman's voice called. A flood of impatient Italian followed.

Andy ran barefoot across to the door and swung the bench aside. Silhouettted against the golden light was an old woman, clutching an ebony stick. "Er . . . *buon giorno* . . ." he stammered feebly.

The others sprang up. Max hung back a little. He liked to be properly dressed. This woman, thought Karen, was as old as his grandmother, and looked, with her strong-boned features and straight-backed carriage, just as formidable.

She was more genial, however. Having sized them up she dropped into broken English – with an American ring, though very different from Mrs Vandyke's precise enunciation.

"You are camping, yes? I disturb you. But last night I lose Nero, and still this morning he does not return—"

"He's *beautiful*," said Karen. "Is he called after the emperor?"

The woman looked blank. "He is called Nero because in Italian that means 'black'. Who is this emperor?"

"He was the very wicked one." Karen remembered how he had thrown Christians to the lions.

"Certainly my Nero is wicked!" She cackled. "But not an emperor. Though he acts like he was." The cat stalked away as if resenting this criticism.

His mistress peered round the schoolhouse. "You are not comfortable. Is not possible." She poked her stick into the straw.

"Oh, we're fine. It's clean and—"

"But not, as you say, 'all the conveniences'!"

"Too right," said Julie.

"Perhaps you could tell us, signora—" Andy began.

"I am called always Donna Margherita."

"Oh . . . er . . . sorry, Donna Margherita. I was going to ask – is there another village near here, with shops?"

"For shops you must go to Cosenza."

"Oh." They looked at each other in dismay.

"For Cosenza there is a bus." She gestured. "Over the top of the hill – after half an hour – you come to the main road. But for today you have missed the bus. It goes very early, to take people to work in the city. It comes back only in the evening."

They had not bargained for anything like this. If they were going to stay here for a day or two someone would have to trek all the way back to Cosenza for supplies.

Donna Margherita read their thoughts. "You come to my place. I have plenty food." She cut short their polite protests. "I am hungry only for new faces! All these folks move out, but I, I will not quit. To hell with the government! Always he said that, my Sammy, God rest his soul." She crossed herself.

"It's real kind of you," said Max.

"Come when you are ready. You cannot miss my house. The last in the village. Beyond the big cross."

"OK to leave our stuff here?" Julie enquired.

"Bring everything. Safer." Donna Margherita swept to the door. No duchess could have made a more stately exit. "I go now. I feed Nero, then I feed you." The cat trotted after her.

They kept silent until she was out of earshot. Then Julie said, 'I wonder who Sammy was. Husband, I suppose."

"But Italian – or American?" said Max. "Sounds like she's lived in the States."

"She'll tell us in her own good time," Karen said. "She's got a lot bottled up. She wants somebody to talk to."

They washed and dressed, left their straw bedding in case they needed it again, packed and rolled up their sleeping-bags.

"Let's go then," said Andy.

They had no difficulty in finding the house. It was much superior to those they passed on the way up. There was a garden wall with an archway and tall wrought-iron gate. Through its black-painted curlicues they saw the building, long and low, with modern picture-windows. A date over the porch showed that it was only twenty years old.

They were greeted by a dignified Nero and the savour of baking bread mingled with freshly ground coffee. Donna Margherita, now in an apron, led them to a vine-trellised terrace with table and chairs. "Of course, breakfast! The young are hungry always, yes?" No one denied that. "Sit. I fetch."

"Can I help you?" Max followed her indoors.

The rugged panorama was something to remember. The pale blue heights of the Sila filled the distance.

Max came back with a laden tray. Donna Margherita followed with the coffee-pot. There was no milk. "As a child," she said, "I milked goats. Not any more. I am alone, I do not trouble myself. There is no one else in the valley. Now it fits its name."

"What's that?" Andy asked.

"They call it the Valley of the Dead. You will not find that name on your map, signore." She snorted. "Always the government has its own names for everything. But to the folks hereabouts always it is the Valley of the Dead. And so it is – now."

"Why was it called that originally?" Karen enquired.

"Who knows? I was not born here. I come from another village."

So the old woman *was* of peasant origin. But how did she come to be living in this modern house, speaking English, not perfectly but fluently enough? The answer was probably the late-lamented Sammy, an American no doubt, who had taken her to the States at some time, though like so many Italians she had come back to end her days in her own country.

And the local people called this the Valley of the Dead. A suitable name, thought Karen. It *was* rather sinister. She had felt that last night. Only on this sun-dappled terrace, with the clink of cups and saucers, the sinister atmosphere was less evident.

"They all said that I must go, that not possibly could I stay. The government . . ." Donna

Margherita gave her opinion on all governments in crude language that Karen knew but would not herself have used. Presumably it had been picked up from Sammy. Karen dared not meet the eyes of her friends who were struggling to choke down their laughter.

"What do your own family think?" she asked politely.

"My own family? I finish with them. Long ago!"

"The government says you must go?"

"They send me letters. A policeman brings them – there is no postman any more. Pah! I tell them what to do with their letters."

"I can believe that," murmured Julie.

"They cut off the electricity. No matter. I have my lamps. Plenty oil. I cook as we did when I was a child." She waved her brown hand at the unkempt garden. "Plenty wood. I am OK."

The house stood so high that they could see the dam beyond the bend in the valley. "I think," Andy said slowly, "you'll be well above the water-line even when the reservoir is filled."

"I know! Why then must I quit? They say, 'health', and 'hygiene'." She almost spat out the words. "They want no one live here no more. They wish *make* it the Valley of the Dead."

"Governments—" began Max sympathetically.

"Governments are not the worst. Others tell me to go – they try to frighten me—"

"Others? Karen echoed. "What others?"

The old woman shook her head. "Is better I say nothing. Forget it. I am not afraid." But you are, you know, thought Karen, for all your defiant tone.

Their hostess seemed determined to change the subject. She asked them about their own homes and families. When they got on to Andy and Karen's studies at college she was clearly out of her depth, until, at the mention of Art, her face lit up.

She smiled at Karen. "You want to be painter?"

"I'm afraid I haven't the talent – I'm not creative. I'm doing History of Art."

Donna Margherita stood up. "I show you my Sammy's pictures. Wonderful pictures!"

She led the way indoors. It was a disappointingly ordinary modern house, characterless in furnishing and decor. No startling experimental paintings, no authentic old peasant craftwork, nothing individual, collected with love and knowledge.

An open staircase led up out of the big living-room to a balustraded landing. At the top Donna Margherita opened the first door with a flourish. "This was his studio!"

It was the biggest disappointment of all. Karen had hoped for lots of pictures hung on the walls or propped against them.

There were a few cheap reproductions in frames. The rest were only pages cut from glossy magazines, pasted on cardboard and hung from nails.

Artistically they were nothing. Run-of-the-mill, commercial stuff, competent and colourful but uninspired. The first showed a cluster of laughing peasant girls, slapping and pounding the household linen on the boulders of a mountain stream. One saucy face was turned towards the artist. Flashing white teeth, red lips, dark eyes dancing . . .

"The first of his pictures I ever saw," said the old woman.

There was another – of the same girl, in regional costume. Red and gold cap on dark curls, full white sleeves with some traditional pattern, a wine-red skirt, grey apron, purple sash.

There were several other pictures of her – standing, lazily outspread in the shade of a cypress, crouching to study her reflection in a pool. None of these was in costume, either festive or everyday.

"Did he paint anything else?" Julie asked. A mischievous chuckle lurked behind her innocent tone. "Landscapes? Mountains and things?"

"Oh, yes, plenty mountains. But mountains I can see through my windows, all the time."

Karen said, "Have you any of the originals?" As Donna Margherita looked blank, she added, "The canvases – the actual paintings?"

The old woman's eyebrows shot up. "How should I? Sammy painted pictures to sell, not hang on his own wall."

And I bet they *did* sell, thought Karen, the luscious nudes anyhow. You might not find Sammy's work in famous galleries but the reproductions would hang in thousands of homes. It would have been commercial all right, in its day, even if popular taste had now moved on.

Donna Margherita's next words confirmed her

guess. "Lucky he could sell them, many, many. That woman! Always she demand more money."

Max swung round. "What woman?"

"That goddam woman in America. His wife."

There was an awkward pause. Karen hoped that Max would not blurt out any more tactless questions. Things were becoming clear enough.

Their hostess faced them with a challenging expression. "You do not see who this girl is? I prove to you." She marched out of the room.

"She doesn't need to," Julie murmured weakly.

Andy said, ungallantly, "Well, if she's going to strip off now, it won't prove anything."

Donna Margherita returned. She carried a hanger from which hung the wine-red skirt, along with the apron, the sash, and the rest of the regional costume. In her free hand she clutched the black slippers and the pointed cap.

It gave the girls something they could genuinely admire and exclaim over as they examined the materials and the exquisite needlework. They were thankful then to escape downstairs again. "She must have been a good-looker when she wore all that," Andy admitted in an undertone.

"Now," announced their hostess. "I make the meal!"

"Anything we can do?" the girls asked.

"Sure!" A shallow basket was thrust into Karen's hand. "Fetch us some fruit from the garden. Peaches – anything that is ripe. The young men help you. And you, Julie – you lay the table, yes? I show you everything."

The others went down into the garden. They

could talk freely now as they searched for ripe fruit. "I get it," said Andy. "She comes from another village. This American artist comes along, spots her among the other girls, gets her to pose for him—"

"Which wouldn't go down well with her family," said Karen, "especially fifty or sixty years ago."

"I expect there was a show-down with her parents—"

"Looks like his wife divorced him in America," said Max, "so he'd have to sell even more pictures to pay her alimony. We don't know if he married Margherita."

"I think she'd wear a ring if he did. So I imagine he didn't," said Karen.

"Why ever not?" Andy demanded. "They stayed together."

"The Church won't marry divorced people. And I bet she's a devout Catholic."

The basket was full. They took it up to the kitchen. "You would like to wash up now?" asked Donna Margherita.

Karen was nonplussed. It seemed a little premature as they hadn't eaten yet. "Of course," she said, polite but mystified.

Max came to her aid. He murmured, "She means what you British mean when you say 'have a wash'." Julie, already quite at home, said, "C'm on, Karen. I'll show you."

The bathroom was tiled, the plumbing was modern and worked, except that there was no hot water and the cold tap dribbled in a rather feeble way. "They couldn't cut that off," Julie explained, "the house has its own tank at the top of the garden. But someone *is* dead set on getting her out. She's scared, y'know, underneath."

"Poor old dear!"

"Not quite my notion of an 'old dear'. Tough as old boots. But I am sorry for her. I think she'd love us to move in here for a night or two. She says she's got lots of empty rooms. Sammy always wanted friends to stay."

"Sammy seems to have been . . . sociable," said Karen darkly. "If she does ask us, it's OK with me."

"I can fix Andy. As for our Maxie – can you imagine him refusing a civilized bed?"

Lunch was simple but substantial, just right for their young appetites. The soup was made from tomatoes grown in the garden, with floating bits of pasta and a sprinkling of grated cheese. The crusty bread was still warm from the old-fashioned oven. The main course was an immense pizza with black olives and dried mushrooms and strips of ham.

They drank local wine from unlabelled bottles. First a dry red with orange tints and a full flavour. "Donnici," the old woman explained, "from our own Montonico grapes. A neighbour used to make the wine for us. Sammy could not learn. And always he prefer his Bourbon whiskey."

With the fruit she produced a white dessert wine, cold from the cellar, deliciously sweet. "Moscato di Cosenza!" she announced. Moscato was made all over Calabria, but, of course, this was the best.

Finally she brought out a box of cigars and seemed disappointed when they were politely declined. She lit one herself, puffing clouds of pungent smoke across the table. It was then that she issued her invitation. If the young people planned to stay in the valley for a few days they must be her guests.

Max was ready briefed for this and answered for them all. "We sure would appreciate that, Donna Margherita, if you're quite certain—"

Her relief was touching. "I have told you – I like to see new faces. Here now, for days, nobody comes. Those who come are those I do not wish to see. Policemen! Officials! Bringing forms and papers. This is better." She drew on her cigar with deep contentment. "Peace," she said.

Just then the afternoon stillness was rudely shattered. From the rocky skyline above them came the thunderous roar of a powerful motorcycle.

# NINE

"Trouble?" murmured Andy.

"Could be," said Max. Was it another official coming to harass Donna Margherita?

She alone seemed in no way alarmed. "It is Furioso. Only he has such a machine, only he would ride that way. But this is not his day to come."

The earsplitting noise ceased at the gate. There were quick booted strides up the path, and a tall black-clad figure appeared, hugging a carton packed with provisions. Above it smiled a craggy face, goggled, beneath a dusty beret from under which peeped grey-white curls.

"Furioso!" cried Donna Margherita with delight.

"Donna Margherita!" The newcomer dumped his burden and swept off beret and goggles together, revealing eyes that twinkled to match his smile. He was wearing a priest's cassock.

Their hostess erupted with a torrent of Italian, gesturing with her cigar as she made the introductions. "Karena, Julia, Andrea, Massimiliano – Maxi!" Then, in English, "This is Don Angeli – though even his bishop calls him Furioso. But you are young, so you treat him with respect."

They all shook hands. "I too speak English a little," said the priest. "I was prisoner of war – in Scotland." His accent betrayed it. "Bonnie Scotland, yes? I was put to work on a farm there." His grey eyes twinkled more than ever. "In

95

Scotland, they told me, the best English of all is spoken."

He sat down. Nero leapt on to his lap, purring with contentment. Donna Margherita went off to fetch another glass.

"I am glad to see you all here," said Don Angeli seriously. "She is too much alone. I try to keep my eye on her, but I have many I must visit. And always – since a lassie – she was so obstinate. We grew up in the same village." He smiled at some memory. "She was a bonnie lassie."

"We imagine so," said Andy, very dead pan. He was thinking, Max guessed, of those pictures.

"She has asked us to stay for a day or two," said Karen.

"Excellent!" He sounded really relieved.

Their hostess returned with a plateful of food and poured him a glass of wine. She slapped down a buff envelope beside it.

He slit it open, drew out a sheet of paper with an official note-heading, put on his spectacles and read it aloud to her. She listened with a contemptuous expression, clucking impatiently at intervals. The others, meanwhile, politely made conversation among themselves.

So, thought Max, she cannot read – she had not even opened the letter until Don Angeli came. Sammy had taken her to the States but she had remained essentially unchanged, an illiterate peasant. Why not, after all? She had not wanted books or newspapers, or to write to the family who had disowned her.

The priest was explaining the letter, advising

her in a patient, earnest tone. She took back the sheet of paper and tore it across.

"Margherita!" He had dropped the "Donna" he had used when he arrived and found her with company. But she was not prepared to discuss the matter further. She turned to Andy, dropping into English again. Don Angeli shrugged his shoulders in despair.

Max saw a chance to satisfy his curiosity. "Can you tell us, Father, why they call this place the Valley of the Dead?"

"It is an ancient tradition. Long ago the peasants dug up many skeletons. It was thought that once there must have been a great battle. Romans – or Saracens."

"A battle?" Andy tried to sound casual. "There were weapons then?"

"Not that I have heard."

"No weapons?" Clearly Andy was wondering, as Max himself was, if the bones could have been those of the wretched labourers, slaughtered by the Gothic chiefs. "How had they died, then?"

"Who knows? This find was made when the Spaniards ruled the country. Perhaps the sixteenth century. There were no archaeologists to puzzle over it." The priest pushed back his chair. "You must excuse, please – I have to hear Donna Margherita's confession and give her communion. I see you again before I go."

The two old people went into the house together.

"Let's make ourselves useful," said Julie.

They cleared the table and took everything into

the kitchen. There was a great pan of hot water on the wood-fired stove. Though the house was modern in other ways Donna Margherita had clearly insisted on the kind of kitchen she had known as a child. It was useless to look round for rubber gloves and detergents.

As they worked they discussed the story of the skeletons.

"It shows we're on the right lines," said Max.

"Could have been plague victims," Karen suggested.

"So far from the city?"

"I suppose not."

"I wonder if he knows just where the skeletons were dug up," said Julie.

"Hardly matters," said Max. "If the Goths wanted to keep the king's tomb secret they'd have been crazy to kill all those poor guys and bury them at the same place."

"You're right," said Andy. "They'd have been marched off somewhere else and liquidated."

"Ugh!" said Karen. "It's like some horror story from World War Two."

It certainly looked as if those vanished skeletons were linked with the Alaric story and confirmed that this was the right valley. In which case it was worth staying here for a day or two, especially as they had been lucky enough to fall in with Donna Margherita.

"But we must find some way to repay her hospitality," Max insisted, "without hurting her pride."

"We'll think of something," said Julie.

He knew she would. She had a knack of getting on with different sorts of people. She'd learnt ways of showing appreciation.

"The next question," said Andy, "is how to get hold of a metal detector."

They could all see that, with their time so limited, it was their only hope of finding whatever it was that Grandfather Vandyke had seen.

"Let's ask Don Angeli," suggested Karen.

Andy considered. "We'd have to tell him the whole story."

"We could trust *him*. You have to trust people or you get nowhere."

"And the old lady would have to know—"

"Sure," said Max. "But she won't let us down."

By the time Donna Margherita and Don Angeli rejoined them on the terrace they had all agreed to put their cards on the table and reveal their motive for coming to this particular valley.

"Alaric?" the priest echoed. "That is another Calabrian legend – I do not know the history." He smiled. "You think, because I am a priest, that I am a man of education? I was a peasant lad when Mussolini made me a soldier. But in Scotland, in the prison-camp, we had a fine chaplain – and I did much thinking as I worked in those fields. I vowed that after the war I would take holy orders. I entered the seminary, I studied theology and Latin and such things. But of most subjects I know little. I remain a simple peasant."

"That is why the people love him," broke in Donna Margherita. "Always he stands up for

99

their rights, always he speaks out when he sees evil – and with a great anger. So he is called Furioso."

"You have to be angry like that sometimes," Karen said.

She was looking at Don Angeli with admiration. Max would have given a lot to catch her looking at *him* like that. Most likely his grandmother would call her a Red. He was sure she'd be a champion of women's rights. That was OK with him. But Grandma wouldn't approve at all.

Andy said, "We were wondering, Father, where we could get hold of a metal-detector. Just for a day or two."

"There are such things in Cosenza. But one cannot go in – as a stranger, indeed a foreigner – and hire one like a bicycle. You need permission from the landowner – and the whole of this valley is owned now by the government. By the time you had filled in the forms—"

"In Italian," murmured Julie.

"We'd be back in England," said Andy pessimistically.

Don Angeli nodded. "And the valley would be under water. Already the programme is several months late. The officials would be unwilling to give you a permit. They are terrified of archaeologists. They would fear still more delay in opening the dam."

"It's hopeless then?"

"No, Andy." The priest chuckled. "I tell you only the regulations. Nothing is hopeless." He produced a dog-eared notebook and tore out a page. He wrote an address and scribbled a few words in Italian. "Matteo Rigoldi is an old friend. He will have such an appliance – he is a builder. His yard is on the way up to the university – ah, I see you have a street-plan, so you will find it easily. I write only 'Please help my young friends if you can.' I do not sign it. Better not. Matteo will know."

"Wow!" cried Karen delightedly. "It's like the Mafia."

"Not at all is it like the Mafia!" Don Angeli rapped out the words sternly, then his expression softened. "I am sorry, lass, you would not understand. The Mafia is a most evil thing. A secret society. Here in Calabria we call it the N'Dranghita. In Naples it is the Camorra. They are all the same thing – a spider's web, a network of crime and murder, blackmail, corruption of every kind."

"I'm sorry, Father. I . . . I was only joking."

"Forgive my anger. I have fought these people for many years. They call themselves also 'the Honourable Society'." He laughed bitterly. "Honourable they are not!"

"The leader in these parts – the 'godfather' – is known as Il Barone," explained Donna Margherita. "He has much power. He got Don Angeli turned out of his parish." Fierce resentment blazed in her eyes. Max had a sudden flash of understanding. She and the priest must be about the same age. Obviously he had known her as a girl. There must be an old, old friendship between them, an indestructible loyalty, even though their lives had taken such different ways.

Don Angeli made light of what she had just said. "I spoke too freely in my sermons. They do not murder priests – that is part of their code – or I should not be here now. But this Il Barone organized a campaign – complaints, anonymous letters to the Bishop—"

"They accused him of most scandalous things! Things I will not say to you young ladies!"

"So they took away my parish. But now there is a new bishop. He has to go carefully, but he has given me work again, a – what do you say? – a roving commission. With my old motorcycle I visit the outlying places. Each week I come to hear Donna Margherita's confession—"

"Also, as you see, he brings my shopping from Cosenza! And all the gossip of the region." She chuckled wickedly.

Don Angeli was obviously keen to explain the full seriousness of the problems caused by the secret society.

"Nothing is too large or too small for these people – if there is money to be made! You are students, yes? If you were at this university you could make sure of passing your examinations. It could be arranged. For a suitable payment!"

In Naples the Honourable Society ran its own illegal football pools, the *toto nero*, or "black tote". But some of the other rackets were far more harmful.

"There is the huge drug traffic. Heroin, cocaine! And then there are the public works."

"Public works?" said Max. That did not sound particularly criminal.

102

For instance, said the priest, Naples had suffered terrible damage in the 1980 earthquake. Reconstruction had cost, in British money, twelve billion pounds. "Ten per cent of that went into the pockets of the Honourable Society."

"How do they do it?" Karen asked.

"Easy. If one construction company will not promise them a bribe, they see that the contract goes to another that will. It is the same in this region. The government allocates huge sums to create work for the unemployed and to open up the country. New roads, new dams, new hydro-electric stations—"

"Like the one here?"

"Yes. Only in this case," said Don Angeli with evident satisfaction, "Il Barone did not manage to fix a cut for himself. So, to teach the contractors a lesson, he has stirred up constant trouble for them. Completion is now a year behind schedule. He has disrupted the delivery of materials, he has organized strikes among the workmen. When the strikes were settled he sent people to frighten the men with superstitious stories – that the valley was haunted, that there was a curse upon the dam." He turned to Donna Margherita. "I have not told you the latest."

"What is that?"

"The watchmen refuse to stay. It is the old story of the *lupomanari* – the watchmen swear that they have actually seen the wolf men. They are quitting. They have been replaced – but I wonder how long the new ones will stay."

"I do not like to hear of the *lupomanari*," said

the old woman uneasily.

"Do not fear." He pressed her hand. To the young people he said, "Donna Margherita clings to the stories of our childhood. She will not believe that this is just another trick of Il Barone. I think it is just a last hopeless fling. After all, the dam is ready. Next month the Minister comes from Rome to declare it open. All the important people, all of what your British soldiers used to call 'the top brass'. After the autumn rains they will have their new lake here. And so, my young friends, you had better make haste. Look for King Alaric's treasure while you can."

"We'll get after that metal-detector tomorrow," Max promised.

# TEN

In the end it was Max who agreed to make the trip back to the city. There was no point in their all going. Andy would be best employed marking out the ground for a systematic search. Julie would stay and help him.

So it fell to Karen to go with Max. The arrangement did not vastly appeal to her. He had fitted into the group better than she had expected, but the instinctive prejudices of their first meeting still lingered. This was the only time, except for the art gallery visits, that they had spent any long period alone together. Which meant, of course, the same for Andy and Julie. At least, she consoled herself, the other two would appreciate a spell on their own.

Donna Margherita woke them early. They must not miss the bus. She had hot coffee ready for them. They gulped it down gratefully, munched a roll, and set off into the dry brilliance of the sunrise. Soon they were over the crest, out of the still shadowed valley, crossing the stony uplands.

Far away to the right loomed the heights of the Sila plateau. Would they ever get there, Karen wondered, see those promised lakes and forests? This treasure-hunt – little more than a joke originally – had taken over the holiday. Andy would not want to move on until they had made a proper search. She herself, much as she had looked forward to the next part of the programme

– Sicily, with its Greek temples and Roman mosaics and its mix of Norman and Arab architecture – had become infected with Andy's determination.

"There's the main road," said Max.

A distant car, like a coloured bead, sped across the arid landscape. Its windscreen flashed a dazzling wink as it caught the sun. As they drew near the highway they could see two black-clad figures sitting beside baskets of produce.

"Haven't missed the bus anyhow," she said with relief.

They greeted the women with a polite *buon giorno* and were answered with wrinkled smiles. Any attempt at real conversation was clearly hopeless.

"They're as inquisitive as hell," Max murmured, "wondering where we've sprung from."

Soon the bus came rattling along. It looked full of workmen and market women, but somehow everybody found room. The air was blue with cigarette-smoke. Donna Margherita's cigars would have been a posy of violets by comparison.

As pervasive as the atmosphere was the curiosity of their fellow-passengers. Several friendly remarks were addressed to them, but for once no one spoke English and their own scanty Italian did not carry them far.

"I think," Karen whispered, "they want to know if we're *married*! Or just good friends."

"Gee!" She could feel the heat from his face so close beside her and a sly glance under her eyelashes confirmed her suspicion. Max had gone very red indeed.

At last the bus pulled up in the middle of Cosenza and they all tumbled out. He looked at his watch.

"I guess the banks hereabouts don't open till nine."

"Do we need a bank?" She was dismayed. They had pooled their Italian currency last night and reckoned that they should have enough.

"Best have plenty of back-up," said Max. "This guy may want a deposit. He may not go much for credit cards. But cash speaks all languages."

"The Vandyke family motto?" she said.

Her sarcastic little digs never seemed to dent his good humour. "Could be," he admitted.

They had an hour to kill. "Let's do the shopping," she suggested. "Get something we can take back to Donna Margherita."

"Fine."

Some shops were taking down their shutters. The market stalls were laid out.

Max had already ruled firmly that they must hire a taxi to run them back. "Can't get this metal-detector thing into a crowded bus. And think of the curiosity! Anyway, we can't hang about all day until the bus goes back this evening."

That was obvious. She just hoped the taxi wouldn't cost the earth. They were supposed to be cheaper abroad. Max, reading her thoughts, said it would be his treat. She felt uncomfortable. It wasn't fair to make snide remarks about the almighty dollar yet accept its benefits when you found it convenient.

With the transport problem solved they felt free

to make their purchases. They bought coffee, chocolates, fancy biscuits, whatever they could imagine would give the old lady pleasure. After a brief debate they added an expensive box of cigars.

"It's against my principles," said Karen.

"I guess nothing we can do will turn her into a non-smoker now," Max argued. "Whatever kills her in the end I reckon it won't be lung-cancer."

"If anything does." Karen laughed. "She looks immortal to me!"

They still had time left for a welcome second breakfast at a café which was just coming to life. They sat under an awning on the pavement, watching the crowds scurrying past to work.

Talk turned to their personal interests and enthusiasms. "History," said Max. There was a wistfulness in his tone. "Now that's what I'd really like to do."

"Has it *got* to be Law?" she said sympathetically. "And Accountancy?"

"I guess so. It's expected – in our family. Later I might . . ."

"Break loose?"

"Maybe. After all I've got brothers. And cousins. I don't see why we *all*—"

"Nor do I. Everyone ought to do his own thing."

"Don't know what my grandmother would say—"

"I do," she said naughtily.

"What?"

"There's no money in History! And she'd be

108

right, of course," Karen added quickly, hoping she had not gone too far. "I'm sure she only wants what's best for you," she ended diplomatically.

"Sure. But, like you said, I guess we've all a right to do our own thing."

The clocks were striking. They finished their coffee and set off for the bank.

There were already a number of customers in front of them. Max let out a little exclamation of disgust.

"What's wrong?"

"Nothing really. Just our old friend from the hotel."

Then she saw his pet aversion, the receptionist. The man was carrying a bulky briefcase and a heavy canvas bag that clinked with small change. Presumably the over-night takings.

His teeth flashed a smile of recognition. He stood aside, waving them to go ahead of him.

"*Grazie*," said Max, but pointed to the section for foreign exchange and strode off towards it.

Karen turned to sit down while she waited, but the man detained her. Perhaps, she thought, he wanted to impress the other customers with his command of English.

"So – you remain still in our city, signorina?"

She never liked hurting anyone's feelings. He must not think that they had moved to a rival hotel. "No," she said, "we're out in the country."

His black brows shot up. "May I ask where?"

No, she thought, that's giving too much away. "We're staying with friends," she answered briefly.

Just then there was a rustle of whispers among the waiting customers. All heads were turned to the street door.

"Il Barone," she caught the words. "Il Barone!"

Two men had entered. One paused and stood, his narrowed eyes ranging over all present, herself included. He looked a proper tough. A strong-arm type, a bodyguard.

His companion was a dapper little man of middle age, smartly tailored. He crossed the tiled floor with swift, almost silent footsteps, ignoring the deferential greetings of the other customers. He headed straight for a closed door at the end of the counter. It opened even before he reached it and was closed by some unseen hand as soon as he had passed through.

As the hotel receptionist was so fond of asking questions she could not resist the temptation to ask him one herself.

"Who on earth was that?"

A warning finger shot up to the fleshy nose. In a shocked whisper came the answer: "That was Luigi Morandi. One of our most respected citizens."

"He looks like it." She escaped at last to a seat. She could see that Max had finished his business at one desk and had moved along to draw the actual cash from another. It looked a lot. But of course even a thousand lire was not very much.

He came back to her, stuffing the wad into his pocket. Normally, she knew, he kept most of his money in a bodybelt next the skin, but he could hardly start undressing in the bank. Anyhow, he might be needing the money in a few minutes.

Talk of "undressing" – there was no other word for the look she got from the muscular body-guard waiting by the door. She was getting used to the shamelessly appreciative glances she constantly received from the young Italians – "they're nicely meant," Julie would say charitably – but this was nothing but a lewd leer. She looked away, avoiding the insolent eyes.

Outside in the street Max's eye was instantly caught by something quite different: an imposing, if over massive, limousine drawn up to the kerb.

"Wonder whose that is? Bullet-proof, I'd reckon."

"Did you see that man in the bank?"

"The thug by the door? I'd like to have given him a poke on the nose." Max sounded quite unusually aggressive. Karen warmed to him.

She laughed. "Glad you didn't!" She winced inwardly, imagining the probable consequences. "No, I mean the VIP who marched straight through to the back as if he owned the place. I've a feeling that it's his car and that he's the man Don Angeli is up against."

"The secret society boss? Il Barone?"

She nodded. "Our hotel friend said he was Luigi Morandi. 'One of our most respected citizens.'" She mimicked his obsequious tone. "Incidentally, our smarmy friend was fishing to find out where *we're* staying now. I just said, 'in the country, with friends.'"

"I'm afraid I had to tell the bank—"

"Oh, the bank's different."

"Sure."

They set out, with Andy's street-plan in hand, to find the address Don Angeli had given them. The university was an unmistakable landmark. It sprawled across the hill in front of them, massive tiers of unlovely concrete, nineteen-seventyish but already weather-blotched and decrepit. It was in sad contrast with the imperial castle crowning the other hill, with its ancient cathedral and picturesque old houses below.

"Here we are," said Max, pausing at the entrance to a builder's yard. A big-bellied, jovial man was checking a consignment of drainpipes. He faced them with an unshaven smile.

"*Buon giorno!*"

"*Buon giorno, signore,*" they said together, and Max added, "*Il Signore Rigoldi?*"

"*Si, si, signore!*" The bald head nodded vigorously, the long brown finger tapped the grubby singlet in confirmation.

Max held out the priest's note. Signor Rigoldi frowned at the brief unsigned message, then eyed his callers shrewdly.

"Don Angeli," said Karen. "Furioso," she added.

"Ah!" The smile returned. "Furioso! Furi-o-so!" He almost sang the name, like a phrase from an opera. He beamed at them. He spread his huge work-worn hands, open palms upwards, in a gesture that seemed to say, what is your pleasure, all that I have is yours!

It was quickly evident that Don Angeli, in his discretion, had omitted not only his identity but any explanation of the help they wanted.

This raised a slight problem, for they did not know the Italian for metal-detector and the word was not in Max's phrase-book. Max however rose to the occasion with a resourcefulness Karen had to admire.

He riffled through the pages, found *I have lost my camera*, and began to read it aloud with a painstaking attempt at the Italian pronunciation. He omitted the last word and mimed "ring" instead, running one of his fingers round another to make sure that he was understood.

"Ah!" Signor Rigoldi was not dumb. Instantly he was all comprehension and concern, though (Karen noticed) it was her own ringless hand not Max's that focused his interest. He became almost fatherly.

Max meanwhile was excelling himself in mime. He donned imaginary headphones, he paced the cobbled yard, he swung his invisible appliance to left and right. He stopped, as though arrested by an inaudible bleep, he bent down, and with an exaggerated cry of triumph, picked up a non-existent ring and slipped it on to his finger.

"*Bravo!*" Signor Rigoldi had watched this performance entranced. He clapped his hands silently. He mimed the tumultuous applause of a crowded theatre. Then he vanished into his work-shop.

"Brilliant!" said Karen.

"I think he's got the message."

The builder had. Also fortunately, he had got a metal-detector, with which he now reappeared. It was just as Andy had described it to them – a long handle, with a circular search-head at one end and an oblong control-box near the hand-grip. There were headphones and a short cable.

Signor Rigoldi demonstrated. Seizing a broom, he swept a patch of the yard clear of fallen nails and other metallic distractions. He removed his own ring and laid it carefully down. The headphones he did not trouble with. Andy had explained that they were needed only if the objects were buried beneath the surface.

They watched intently. The control-box had a needle, which the builder centred carefully before starting. It could swing left to green, right to red. When he switched on, there was a tuning note, not very loud, maintaining a continuous pitch.

To and fro he paced, sweeping the search-head low over the cobbles. As it passed over the ring there was a break in the pitch. He swung the search-head back, holding it directly over the ring. The sound steadied again, but the note was now markedly different, reverting to the original sound when the detector moved away.

Signor Rigoldi brought it back over the ring. Again came the break in pitch, the altered note. He beckoned them closer, pointing to the needle. It had swung over to the red section of the arc.

"*Oro!*" he explained. He put the gold ring back on his finger, then dropped an iron key a few paces in front of him. Again the constant tone of the detector broke and changed as it hovered over the key, but this time the needle had swung round to green.

"*Ferro,*" he said.

"It's cute," said Max. "It knows the difference all right."

It did not take long to complete the transaction. Max indicated that they wished to hire the detector for three days. He produced a wad of notes from which the builder peeled off a modest sum. There seemed to be no question of a deposit. When Max tried to indicate his readiness to pay one the builder seemed almost shocked, though in a most benevolent way. "Furioso," he said, shaking his head and patting Max's shoulder. "Furi-o-so!" Any friend of Don Angeli clearly needed no further guarantee.

It was now just a question of returning in triumph to their friends.

"*Automobile?*" queried Signor Rigoldi, glancing out into the street.

"No, signore – taxi," said Karen. With luck, she thought, he'll be kind enough to call us one.

But he had other ideas. "*Taxi? Non!*" His eyes rolled in comical horror as he added in shocked tones, "*Furioso!*" Meaning, presumably, that Furioso would be furious if they were put to such expense.

He strode across to a battered-looking old truck and carefully dusted the seat. "*Prego!*" He bowed with a courtesy that would have gone well with velvet breeches and powdered wig. He handed her up. Max climbed in after her. The metal-detector was lifted carefully into the back and Signor Rigoldi took the driving seat.

His eyebrows shot up when they gave him the name of the village, but when Karen added

"Donna Margherita" it seemed to make everything instantly comprehensible.

They drove out. As the city outskirts fell behind them Signor Rigoldi burst into a full-throated rendering of *La donna e mobile*. The famous aria from *Rigoletto* conquered even the thunderous racket of the truck.

# ELEVEN

They found Andy and Julie down by the river. Indeed, Julie was *in* the river. There were warm shallow pools between the rocks, where one could lie back luxuriously, contemplating one's brown legs in the gently wavering water.

They had thrust sticks into the ground, marking out the possible area with lengths of white tape which Andy had thoughtfully brought from England.

"Must be systematic," he said. "No sense in searching the same bit twice."

Julie yawned like a bored mermaid. "Not much sense in searching it even once, if you ask me," she murmured for Karen's ears alone. Julie's enthusiasm had soon evaporated in the heat of the morning.

But not Andy's. He had greeted Max and Karen with delight. "You've got it? Great! Now we can really get busy." He checked the metal-detector to satisfy himself that it was in working order. He was, thought Karen, like a small boy with a new mechanical toy.

"Have a heart!" Julie protested. "These two have only just got back. And carrying this contraption! They must be about bushed."

"Suppose we take an early lunch-break?" said Max tactfully.

They had already handed over the bulk of their shopping to Donna Margherita, who had accepted the ordinary provisions with a good grace, the little luxuries with profuse thanks, and the cigars with positive ecstacy. Karen had, however, taken out the ingredients for a picnic here, so that they need not climb up to the house again in the heat of midday.

"The old girl seems real glad to have us around," said Julie. "I was talking to her this morning. She doesn't give away much. But I got a feeling."

"Must be lonesome," Max said, "with only the cat."

"She strikes me as so tough and – well, self-sufficient," said Karen.

"She's got used to being alone," her cousin agreed. "Sammy died five years ago. Just as we thought, they were never able to marry. And because he wasn't a Catholic he had to be buried in a separate corner of the churchyard."

"Another reason why she doesn't want to leave here."

"And the house itself. Sammy had it built for her, she was so homesick to come back to Italy."

"And now all the neighbours have quit," said Max.

"I don't think she cared much about them," said Julie. "Remember, this was never *her* village. But she couldn't go back there – ever. Her own folks had broken with her. She was the no-good girl, the one who went off with the foreign painter. She *is* self-sufficient, she'd have been quite happy to stay on here alone—"

"But for the dam?" Karen suggested.

"Not just that. After all, the water isn't going to come up this high. I think it's all the different pressures being put on her—"

"These government forms," said Max. "She can't even read them."

"It's not just those, either. I'd back Donna Margherita against any of these officials."

Andy joined in. "Julie thinks someone else is putting the frighteners on her."

Karen remembered what Don Angeli had said about Il Barone, who had obstructed the dam project because the contract had not gone to the company he favoured. Il Barone had "put the frighteners" on the superstitious workmen. Even now, he was still trying to scare away the watchmen.

Where would Donna Margherita fit into that scenario? What motive had he for frightening *her* away? As an obstinate house-owner, refusing to budge from the valley, surely she'd be an asset in his campaign against the scheme. Somehow it didn't hang together.

"She's real scared by something," Julie insisted. "Especially after dark."

"Well," Karen said, "only two nights ago she was wandering about in the middle of the night."

"How do you know?" They all stared at her.

"It was the night we slept in the school. I heard some weird noises – I realized, the next morning, when we met her, it was the special call she has for Nero. If she was out and about at that hour she couldn't have been all that scared."

"Love casts out fear," said Andy humorously

but with a hint of impatience. He'd finished eating. He wanted to get on with the search.

Max was more sympathetic to Karen in her perplexity. "Maybe something fresh has happened to worry her. Something we don't know about."

Andy jumped up. "If it's something we don't know, we can't do much about it. Anyhow, she'll be OK till dark. If we don't get started soon we'll have lost another day."

The deep valley was now a cauldron of heat. Andy and Max were stripped to the waist. The girls wore only their bikinis, braving the thorny bushes and the insects. When the heat became unbearable they picked their way back to the river-bank and slipped into a pool.

They took turns with the detector. It was not heavy, though in time one's arm ached with holding it at the right level, just clear of the ground. One soon tired, too, of the headphones clamped over one's ears, but it was no use searching without them. They were looking now for things hidden in the earth under the weeds and stones.

"How deep does it go?" Max asked.

"About a metre," said Andy, "if it's something a fair size. Smaller things – like coins – have to be nearer the surface to register."

So if everything's really deep, thought Karen gloomily, it won't show up at all. Those objects Mr Vandyke had seen might be six feet under by now or even deeper, after all that bombing.

Andy remained optimistic. "We've just got to find one thing, to give us a lead. Then we can dig round it."

Donna Margherita had lent them garden tools to add to the abandoned implements they had salvaged from the village. They had trowels and a little hand-fork now, vital for more delicate work if they really did make a find. You had to be so careful in archaeological digging. Even a metal helmet might, after centuries in the earth, be wafer thin. A spade or shovel, used too vigorously, could work havoc.

After several hours the area still to be searched looked dauntingly extensive. Andy had drawn a plan to scale, based on the alignments of church and calvary as Max's grandfather might have seen them, according to where he was. The plan showed a shaded area stretching from the modern river-bank to the first houses of the village. The crater must have been somewhere in that area, it could not possibly have been outside, for nowhere else would the two landmarks have come into line.

Looking from the diagram to the actual stretch of ground it represented, Karen calculated with a sinking of the heart that they might have three days of this toil and sweat in front of them.

They worked short spells each, or they lost concentration. Andy was a stern taskmaster. "You've got to pass the search-head over every inch of the strip you're doing. Better to overlap and test a bit twice over than get too light-hearted and miss a vital patch. Thorough, that's the motto!"

"That's what I admire about men," Julie snarled under her breath. "*Thorough!* Grrrh!" There seemed little risk of Julie's becoming too light-hearted.

It was Karen, however, who got the first positive reaction from the detector.

"Hi!" she yelled suddenly. "Funny noise!"

They came racing over.

She held out the headphones to Andy. "You listen." She thrust the long handle into his eager fingers.

"You're *right*!" He moved the search-head to and fro, his face transfigured. "It's broken pitch! It's steady again now . . . but it's a different note."

Karen remembered the meter and peered at it. The needle had swung round and was quivering in the green half of the arc.

"Only ferrous," she said, disappointed.

"Never mind," said Max. "There's something there, anyhow."

Andy moved a few paces. The others could hear nothing, only guess from his expression what signal he was receiving through the headphones. At last he said, "There's a lot of stuff all round here. Wherever I move, I get this different sound." He let them listen in turn. Then he laid the detector aside and picked up the garden fork. "Let's try here."

Max grabbed the spade, but Andy made a warning sound and he put it down again.

Andy probed the ground with a surgeon's delicacy. Having gentle loosened the top soil he knelt down with a trowel, scraping. They held their breath.

"Something hard here." He brushed away the earth with his fingers. "Round." He paused. They saw a few inches of curved surface, caked with khaki dust, but unmistakably metal.

Karen exclaimed. "It's a helmet!"

"It looks marvellously well preserved." There was a doubt in Andy's voice. "Here we are!" The helmet came out, dribbling the dry powdery soil.

Only it was not, unfortunately, a helmet. It was an old-fashioned cooking-pot – old enough to be thrown away, not nearly old enough to rank as archaeological.

There was a general gasp of disgust. "Early twentieth century, I guess," said Max, joking to cover his own disappointment. "They used to make things to last, more than we do."

"It doesn't mean there isn't something much older close by," Andy argued. "You always get modern things lying on top of earlier layers."

Karen knew it happened all the time on archaeological digs. But her enthusiasm had taken a knock.

Andy started probing carefully again, but not so carefully as before. He did not check his friends when they began a little investigating themselves.

After half an hour their labours had been rewarded – if rewarded was the word – with a brass army buckle, two broken-bladed knives, some scraps of old harness and miscellaneous rubbish of all kinds. When they came upon the rusty frame of a bicycle there could be no doubt about the significance of their discovery. They had located not the priceless hoard of the Gothic king but a rubbish-dump dating back only a few years.

Fate's final tactless joke was a horseshoe. "Good luck, I *don't* think," said Andy sourly.

They agreed to call it a day. The valley was now all in shadow, only the rugged skyline suffused with a warm apricot glow. The air was suddenly chilly. The Valley of the Dead was taking on again its more sombre aspect.

Rather wearily they trudged up the village street. "We'll have another go tomorrow," said Andy, and they murmured agreement. They mustn't give up. The rubbish-dump had been a disappointment but it had been an obvious possibility. People often threw away their stuff like that, somehow assuming that it would all be washed away by the winter floods.

Nero welcomed them back, winding between their legs, a friendly furry rub for each. Donna Margherita seemed equally pleased to see them. Alluring odours of supper floated from the kitchen.

When the meal was over, and their hostess puffing contentedly at a cigar, Karen described her brief glimpse of Il Barone in the bank.

"Of course they all showed him respect!" said the old woman tartly. "They are all so scared of him." She did not sound scared of him herself. "It does not pay to get across Il Barone." She tossed her grey head. "Some have tried. Ask them how they made out. They cannot tell you. Because they are dead!"

Countless murders, she explained, were carried out on his orders. Sometimes the killings were public, in daylight, in the street. A bullet – full in the face at close range – was the favourite method for an important enemy or for a traitor who had betrayed the Honourable Society. That was because Il Barone had to demonstrate his power.

In other cases he might not want publicity. So the victim would simply disappear and never be seen again.

"That way we call 'the white shotgun'," said Donna Margherita grimly. "The body is simply thrown into wet concrete. With all these new roads and bridges there are always big holes being filled with concrete. This dam they have built here – how many of Il Barone's enemies lie buried in it? Who will ever know?"

It was spine-chilling. "Aren't *you* afraid of him?" said Karen.

"I? No. The Honourable Society does not kill women. I do not think even he would break that rule. Likewise he cannot kill Furioso, because he is a priest. Though he would be glad enough to see Furioso dead. Always Furioso tell the people to stand up to him, always Furioso expose him and his dirty rackets. But I . . ." She shrugged. "I am just harmless old woman. I mind my business."

Clearly Julie's impression had been correct. Whatever was troubling their hostess she did not seem to be intimidated by Il Barone.

It was soon time to think of bed. It had been a long day for all of them. Donna Margherita opened the door for Nero. Karen stepped out into the moonlight, eager to fill her lungs with the cool garden-scented air after all that cigar-smoke. Donna Margherita called after her.

"Do not go into the garden! Is not – safe. You could fall in the dark—"

"But the moon's as bright as day!"

"Better you not go! There might be . . ." The old woman hesitated. "Snakes," she said feebly.

"OK." Karen took one more deep breath, gazing round that spectral landscape, silver-grey and savage under the moon's sharp radiance. She returned indoors, Nero padding behind. Donna Margherita shot the bolts decisively. Taking their lighted candles, as in Victorian days, they all filed upstairs.

Sleep came quickly after the labours of the day. But by midnight Karen was wide awake again.

Downstairs there was a loud, measured knocking on the door.

# TWELVE

"What on earth . . .?" gasped Julie from the other bed.

Radiant moonlight slanted through the unshuttered window. Karen saw her cousin's eyes, wide and startled. She was startled herself.

"Police?" she murmured.

"This hour o' night?"

Karen padded to the window and cautiously peered down. As she expected, there was no one on the terrace. To see the front door meant going to the top of the stairs – and even then there would be the porch.

There was no more knocking, yet no sound of the door being opened. That was odd. Whoever had taken the trouble to come to this isolated house would surely knock again. Could Donna Margherita possibly have slept through the noise?

Apparently not. There were footsteps on the landing.

"I hope she won't open up," said Julie, "unless she knows who it is."

"Better show we're around." Karen opened the bedroom door.

Donna Margherita had nearly reached the head of the stairs. She made an eerie figure against the bright oblong of the window. Her long grey hair straggled loose, unkempt. But when she turned to face the girls she would not have frightened any one. She looked terrified herself.

She laid her finger on her lips. "We must not answer the first knock!"

They stared, bewildered. Then came the second knocking. Nor urgent or impatient. Measured. Portentous.

"Nor the second time!" The old woman's hand was like carved ivory as she gripped the rail, blocking the way down.

Karen was not at all anxious to go down anyhow. She stepped to the window.

"Do not look!"

"Why not?"

"He is changing shape! At the first knock one sees only a wolf. At the second knock a man – but still with the head of a wolf. At the third knock only a man. You must not look yet!"

That kind of order Karen found impossible to obey. She must see. Heart in mouth she leant over the window-sill. In the full moonlight outside the porch stood a motionless figure.

Her heart nearly stopped. It was true. The figure was human – but the head upturned to meet her incredulous stare was the head of a wolf. She drew back with a little scream.

"Here, let *me*!" Andy was at her elbow. Max behind him. A vast relief swept over her. Later she recalled with amusement that even at this dramatic moment Max had paused to slip on his wonderful silk dressing-gown, while Andy's bare back gleamed like a statue as he craned out into the silver night.

Again that knocking!

"I'll fix him, whoever it is." Andy withdrew his

head.

"You must not go down, Andrea!" Donna Margherita's arms stretched out to stop him. But Andy was not trying to go down. He ran back into his bedroom.

A blood-curdling voice began to declaim from outside. Karen could not make out a word. It was probably in the old Calabrian dialect anyhow. The old woman kept sobbing, "*No! No!*" Defiant, yet desperate.

Andy came racing back. He shoved Max aside. He was clutching something. Karen saw his shoulder jerk as he threw.

There was a howl from below. Not a wolf's howl, but a very human one. The threatening voice was heard no more. Only a scuttle of booted footsteps fading.

Andy swung round, almost colliding with Donna Margherita. "Do not open the door!" she screamed, but he brushed past her. Max followed him downstairs. The girls, their fear forgotten, were close behind.

Andy unbarred the door. Outside, the garden spread empty and silent. He ran out and picked up a small lump of rock with a cry of satisfaction. Karen recognized it as a treasured geological specimen he had collected near Vesuvius.

"You hit him," said Max admiringly.

"Sounded like it."

"Good shot!"

"I've played a lot of cricket," he said modestly. He had something in his other hand. He held it up in triumph as Donna Margherita joined them.

"The gentleman forgot his hat."

It was a brown hood with eyeholes. It had pointed ears stitched on and a long padded snout.

Their hostess cried out in relief. "Furioso was right then. It *was* only a man dressed up! I was an old fool to believe such stories."

She barred the door again, then led the way into the kitchen and stirred the hot ashes into a ruby glow. They were all too wide awake to return to bed immediately. She threw fresh wood on the fire and warmed some red wine in a saucepan, sprinkling in sugar and spices. They fetched extra clothes and gathered round the blaze.

"When I was a child," said Donna Margherita, "I heard terrible tales of the *lupomanari*. But it is only lately that folks say they have seen them."

"Since the dam was started?" Max asked.

She considered. "I guess so. Not till then."

Karen remembered that nightmare drawing in the school desk. She remembered too what the priest had told them. "Wasn't it a trick of Il Barone? To scare away the workmen?"

"Furioso said so. But I did not believe him. Nor did the workmen. Many quit. The job was at a standstill. Then the contractor brought in men from the North who laughed at our Calabrian superstitions. Yet people in this village swore that they had seen the wolf-men." Clearly, thought Karen, Il Barone had gone to a lot of trouble.

"But the dam *was* finished," she said.

"Behind time. Ten months."

"I don't see the sense—"

"I do," said Julie. "There's a penalty clause in

contracts. If the construction firm doesn't meet the deadline they have to pay. If it's a long delay they can lose a hell of a lot of money." Julie was always coming out with odd scraps of information she'd picked up in her temporary jobs.

Donna Margherita nodded agreement. "Revenge," she said. "Il Barone cannot afford to be beaten in anything. In this country honour matters. A man must take revenge or he counts for nothing."

"But it doesn't explain why they should come bothering *you*," said Julie. "What was that character shouting outside?"

"That I should leave this house. The valley is haunted."

"Well, you won't believe that now," said Andy, "not after this!" He swung the wolf-mask scornfully in his hand.

"But why should *they* want you to go?" Julie persisted. "The government, yes – they don't want people living above the reservoir. But why should this gangster and his thugs mind?"

"Anyhow," said Karen, "the dam's going to be opened now – the bigwigs are coming down for the ceremony – in a few weeks, isn't it?"

"The first of September," said the old woman. "Unless something happens," she added darkly.

"What *can* happen? Now?"

"Who knows? But – I tell you – Il Barone cannot afford to be beaten."

Max was looking very thoughtful. "Let's suppose this guy is still planning something. He doesn't want any witnesses around right now.

131

Not even a harmless old lady—"

"I am *not* a harmless old lady!" The retort came sharp as a pistol-shot. Max winced.

"I'll say you're not," he admitted.

The first of September, Karen was thinking. By then they would be back in England, their Inter-Rail tickets expired, college term looming for Andy and herself. They had agreed to allow three more days for the treasure-hunt. Then, if (as likely) they'd found nothing, they must move on to Sicily and the rest of their programme. But even if they scrapped their programme and stayed on here, there was no way they could keep Donna Margherita company until the dam was opened. If only Don Angeli could persuade her to go away for a few weeks until the vital date was past! What a hope, she told herself, knowing the old woman's obstinacy.

The spiced wine made a splendid nightcap after all the drama. They trooped upstairs again, yawning. While Andy and Julie were saying goodnight Max turned to Karen. "Sleep tight, nothing to worry about. Andy and I will take turns on watch till it gets light."

"You *are* good," she said, and meant it.

There were no more alarms. The wolf-man did not return to face more missiles.

After breakfast they went straight down to the river to start work while the valley-bottom was still cool with shadow. They worked in pairs, so that one couple could relax at will while the other moved to and fro with the detector.

Inevitably Max and Karen were partners again.

132

But continuous conversation was impossible, for the person wearing the headphones had to listen carefully for any break of pitch. There were momentary excitements when some worthless scrap of modern metal provoked the warning signal. Otherwise it was a monotonous job.

They had brought a picnic lunch again. They sat by the little river, the cicadas keeping up their shrill incessant chorus, the water chuckling over the pale stones.

They had made good progress. They could now move the white tapes and mark out narrow strips of the middle area, halfway to the nearest houses.

"The most promising area, this," said Andy, "to judge from what Max's grandfather told us."

Andy and Julie took the next spell. Karen and Max sprawled in the shade. It was possible to talk properly now, but both were drowsy with the heat and the sleep they had lost during the night. Karen had to shake Max when the hour was up. Must play fair with the others. They had all agreed, single-hour stretches were better than longer spells. Easier to maintain concentration.

No false alarms enlivened their next shift. To and fro they paced, the sweat beading their skin. The detector never varied its pitch. It was a relief to remove the pressure of the hot earphones, feel the air, and hear the cicadas again. When Andy and Julie came over to take their turn it was bliss to return to the river and slip into the water.

If Grandma Vandyke could only see her pet grandson now, thought Karen. Dear Maxie's unshaven chin showed the beginnings of a presentable beard. Mrs Vandyke would have said he was turning into a proper layabout. That long hair, too!

Karen, on the contrary, would have said that Max was beginning to look quite human. Indeed, he reminded her of those youths painted on ancient Greek vases. He was not as muscular as Andy, admittedly, but she was not a girl who got all that excited by muscle.

These agreeable thoughts, as she lay drying on the grass, were interrupted by a distant yell from Julie. They both sat up and saw that Andy was signalling excitedly.

"Probably another rubbish-dump," said Karen, but she could not help hoping.

They raced across to see. Andy was working over a rough uncultivated patch. "How about this?" he demanded. In his palm lay a small mud-coated coin. The edge glinted yellow. "Feel it," he said. "It won't break. It must be gold."

Julie was on her knees, scrabbling in the dry soil, for once careless of her well-manicured nails. "There are lots more," she gasped.

Soon they were all frenziedly rubbing coins. They were hard, not worn thin by their time in the earth. As the smeared mud flaked away the metal shone through.

"There's a head on this!" cried Karen.

"And this one," said Max. "Some lettering too. Latin, I guess. *Imp* – that'll be short for *Imperator*!"

Julie was scratching away like a dog in quest of a buried bone. "Something bigger here!"

"Careful then," said Andy. "You could damage it."

But when they had gently loosened up the soil and brushed it aside, the object that came out was as hard and firm as the coins. It was a woman's diadem, a graceful arc of delicately fashioned oak leaves.

They took it to the river and washed away the dirt. With other metals they knew it would not have been safe. Silver would be already corroded by damp. Bronze and copper acquired a patina which protected them, but ignorant amateurs must not remove it. Only gold was incorruptible. Warm soapy water would bring back its pristine brightness. For the moment a rinse in the river must do.

The diadem came out as authentic gold – except for some brilliant green stones set round the edge. Julie polished them with her head-scarf. They winked back in the sun.

"I bet those are emeralds," she said.

"I guess we *have* found something," said Max quietly.

Their pent-up excitement exploded like the opening of a champagne bottle. There were hand-clasps and bear-hugs and kisses as they danced madly round.

# THIRTEEN

Andy was the first to recover his sanity.

After all, thought Max, *he* was always kissing Julie anyhow – and Karen too, though only in a friendly way. For Max himself it was a novel experience and he wished it had gone on longer.

Andy was now thoroughly businesslike. "We'll have to report this at once. There may be a load of stuff under here. The old gadget was going berserk."

"It'll need experts," said Karen. "We certainly mustn't mess it about by ourselves."

"And a police guard. You know what some of these peasants are like. Tomb-robbing is a national industry." Andy surveyed the deserted hillsides. "The news'll get round in no time. They'll appear out of the sky. Like ruddy vultures."

"If only there was a phone," said Julie. "I suppose someone will have to walk into Cosenza."

Max had an idea. "No need. Those watchmen must have a phone at the dam."

"Sure to," Andy agreed. He hesitated. "Would *you* mind ?"

"Glad to."

"Fine."

Max wondered if Karen would offer to go with him. But Andy was already organizing the most urgent jobs. All traces of their digging must be covered over, the spot marked in some way only identifiable by themselves. The white tapes crisscrossing the site must be rolled up. The tools and the detector must be carried up, with the diadem and the coins, to Donna Margherita's house. All activity must then be suspended until the police arrived.

Max picked his way across the river and made for the mule-track by which they had come down on the first day.

"Don't get lost!" Karen called after him.

He waved cheerfully. "What do you take me for? I'll be back before dark." He quickened his pace, though it was breathless work until he had climbed out of the valley and reached the more level motor-road along the crest. From there onwards he made good time.

The watchmen on the dam were not the pair who had stopped them before. They were taller, more confident in manner. Outsiders, maybe, from the North, less likely to be scared by were-wolf rumours. Max greeted them politely. He was learning that Italians appreciated a more cere-monious greeting than was usual between casual Anglo-saxons. Neither of them, unfortunately, spoke English.

"*Telefono?*" he enquired. "*Carabinieri,*" he added to show that he had good reason for his request.

"*Carabinieri?*" Mention of the police alerted them. "*Automobile?*" asked one. He brought his hands together in violent collision and rolled his eyes to suggest the agonies of an injured person.

"*No, no, signore.*" Max shook his head vigor-ously to reassure him that there had not been a car-crash. The watchmen conferred together volubly. They were clearly wondering whether, if it was not a case of accident, they could allow this young foreigner to use their telephone. He caught the word "*importante*" and seized upon it.

'*Si, si! Importante. Molto importante!*" He waved his passport. They showed interest. He laid a currency note tactfully on the table. Their interest grew. "*Telefono*," he pleaded. "*Carabinieri! Importante!*"

They were all smiles and helpful now. One picked up the telephone, dialled, and broke into a torrent of personal greetings. Then came the explanations. "*Americano . . . Si, si, americano . . .*" He held out the instrument to Max.

Thankfully Max heard English from the other end. "There has been an accident, sir?"

"No, no. But there is something that must be notified to the police." Max patiently gave his name and other details.

"And this matter you wish to report?"

He had rehearsed the answer in his mind. Better not mention gold at this stage, still less the treasure of King Alaric. He said, simple, "It is something we have found, my friends and I. It may be of archaeological importance."

"Ah . . . archaeological?" Was that a yawn at the other end?

"It requires expert investigation," he said firmly.

"And where is it, this archaeological discovery?"

"In the valley, upstream from the dam. It is hard to explain." Max became wary. The watchmen were listening but did not look as though they understood the conversation. "We can show you," he said.

"Very well. I will send someone in the morning."

"In the morning? Not today?" Had he gone too far in playing down the urgency of the matter?

"It will be too dark now for any investigation. You have not found anything of great value?"

Max thought he had better not alter his story at this stage. Fatal to give a hint of the possible riches buried in the valley and still find that the Carabinieri could not send out before tomorrow. "No," he said.

"Then it will keep till tomorrow," said the voice comfortably. "Where are you staying, Mr Vandyke?"

He explained. He caught laughter over the wire. "Donna Margherita? The obstinate old lady? Now there is a beauty of antiquity which none of us can dig out!"

The officer seemed at once to regret this lapse into familiarity, for his tone became anxiously correct, and the conversation ended with an exchange of courtesies and a promise that the Carabinieri would be out first thing in the morning.

Max replaced the telephone. The currency note had disappeared from the table. The watchmen saw him to the door and bade him goodnight.

It was by this time almost dark. The moon had not risen, the hills were spectral masses in the dusk. He started briskly along the road. After about a mile he must keep a sharp look-out for the mule-track slanting down to the river.

Ahead, far-off, he heard the faint hum of a car. It was the first sign of traffic on this road. But of course there were no big towns inland, local drivers would be few, and any tourists exploring the Sila would now be back in their hotels, changing for dinner.

It must be a powerful car. Its sound alternately swelled and faded as it followed the twists of the road and vanished briefly behind some bulging mass of mountain. It was coming this way, fast. Its driver knew the road.

Suddenly it was upon him, whipping round a curve, its headlights a white glare. He had to jump aside smartly. The driver clearly did not expect pedestrians. Or have much use for them. He hooted arrogantly as he roared by. Dazzled, stumbling on the uneven verge, Max saw the rearlight shrink to a ruby pin-point and vanish.

Someone impatient to get to Cosenza, he thought, I can't imagine why.

If the driver had been hastening to Cosenza he must suddenly have changed his mind. The roar of the engine was heard again, the bleak landscape stood out under the pallid wavering light, and the car surged past him. This time there was no disdainful hoot.

"Not the kinda guy to offer lifts," Max murmured to himself. As it happened he did not want one. But it would have been all the same if he had been a hitch-hiker with a ten-mile stretch ahead of him.

Ah! With some relief he recognized a pair of cypresses, rising like black spears against the growing glitter of stars. A few yards further would be the mule-track forking to the left. Fine! Here it was.

Since the passing of the car the silence had been broken only by his own footsteps. Now he was suddenly aware of a footfall not his own. Softer. Stealthy.

He spun round. Two figures were almost upon him. They must have been waiting behind the cypresses.

*"Signore . . ."*

The voice was low, muffled, but the note of warning unmistakable. Cold metal ground into his temple. His hands were twisted behind his back. When the grip relaxed he found that he still could not move them. It felt as though they were bound with strong sticky tape.

He tried to shout, but a hand was clamped over his mouth. The smell of nicotine was rank in his nostrils. The gun-muzzle was still pressed hard against his forehead. He ceased to struggle. What help could he hope for on this deserted road?

The man with the pistol wore a hood like the one Andy had picked up, a wolf-mask with pointed ears and muzzle. His companion, similarly disguised, kept a painful, no-nonsense grip on Max's arm. These were no werewolves from another world, but experienced and determined thugs.

They thrust Max forward along the road. Round the next bend stood a long limousine, its lights off, a figure standing beside it.

A voice spoke. In English, with a distinct accent.

"Mr Vandyke Junior, I believe? I apologize for any discomfort – it will not be a long drive – but I fear that for security reasons you must travel in the boot."

The boot? Max remembered – it was what the British called the trunk of an automobile.

He began to protest angrily, but the two wolf-men seized him tightly. He felt himself swung off the ground and thrust down, twisting and kicking furiously, on to a blanket smelling strongly of dog. There was a thud as the lid of the boot shut over him. In that confined space the canine stench was overwhelming. He heard the car doors shut, the engine roar into life. Smoothly the limousine glided forward.

# FOURTEEN

For a long time they did not worry about Max's failure to return.

"It'll be the police," said Julie confidently, "with all their forms and questions. Those weeks I worked for the lawyers – I learnt something about 'police inquiries', believe you me!"

There were so many possible explanations. The Carabinieri might have told Max to wait at the dam until they could get out to him. They might have taken him back into Cosenza. When all the formalities were completed they would probably run him back to Donna Margherita's by the other road. And even if they didn't, Max had the wit – and the money – to pay for a taxi.

It was most unlikely, by now, that he was walking back the way he had gone and there would have been little sense in Andy's setting out in the hope of meeting him half-way. Also, now that night had fallen, they had to think of Donna Margherita. Though she seemed to have quite recovered her indomitable spirit, suppose the wolf-man came again? After dark, for the time being at least, Andy felt that there ought to be a man on the premises.

In the cheerful kitchen, odorous with meat stew and herbs, Max's non-appearance seemed no occasion for great concern. The talk was all of their dramatic discovery. They showed Donna Margherita the diadem and the coins. Sure enough, they needed only warm soapy water to restore the brilliance of over fifteen centuries ago.

The old woman was astounded. But it was not in her nature to be speechless.

"So! This time the stories of my childhood *are* true! All over Calabria they tell tales of lost treasures – and you have found one. A king's treasure, you say?"

They told her about Alaric. Romans and Goths meant little to her. But the jewel-studded diadem – she could wipe her hands on her apron and finger it.

"Max was right to go and tell the Carabinieri. We might all be murdered in our beds. Let the policemen come out and do something useful for once. Why should you children do all that digging in the hot sun?"

Their euphoria turned supper into a celebration. What a shame that Max was missing it all! Karen wished again that Donna Margherita still had a telephone. Max could have rung them and explained the delay. But, of course, if only there had been a telephone he would never have needed to walk to the dam.

As they finished the meal there was a welcome interruption. Don Angeli's motorcycle came thundering down the lane. Donna Margherita hurried off with a swish of black skirts to unbar the door and let him in. They heard her exclamations of welcome. The priest swept into the kitchen, face alight.

"You have good news already, then?"

"Look!" Julie held up the diadem. It flashed and glittered under the lamp.

He took it from her and turned it in his hands. "*Mirabile!* And there is more?"

Andy dribbled the coins on to the table. "Much more, I should think – from the way the detector was behaving. We didn't dig any further. Better to leave it to the experts. After all, if it's Alaric's share from the loot of *Rome*—"

"And perhaps also of Jerusalem, laddie."

The priest's voice had suddenly taken on an almost reverent tone. It went oddly with the homely Scottish word.

"Jerusalem?" They stared.

"You mean the great Temple? Where Jesus himself preached?"

"And kicked out the money-changers?" Karen had always liked that bit.

"Ay. Well, some years after that the Temple was looted by the Roman soldiers. All its treasures were carried off to Rome – the seven-branched lamp-holder that burned the holy oil, the seven silver trumpets of the Jewish priests, the altar of Solomon, the sacred vessels, everything . . ."

Don Angeli might protest that he knew little history and was only a peasant boy trained for the priesthood. But his studies had left him with a vivid impression of the Temple, its central place in Jewish religion, its incredible wealth and splendour. He remembered, too, that this glory had all vanished when the Roman army suppressed the Jewish revolt in AD 70.

"It is depicted on the Arch of Titus in Rome," he said.

"Oh, we saw *that*," Karen remembered. But

who could recall the details of all they had seen in those crowded days?

"I have seen only photographs of the carvings," the priest admitted, "but they show the legionaries carrying off their plunder – the great golden candelabrum, the long silver trumpets, everything. And a few centuries later it was the turn of Rome to be captured and plundered."

"Alaric?" Karen's whisper was tense. She saw the way the story was going.

Don Angeli nodded. "Alaric. After the Goths the Temple treasures were never seen again."

"*Wow!*" said Julie. It was what they all felt. "The Goths?"

"I believe, now I think back, it was what they told us in the seminary. It was the tradition at least. There was no other way to explain what had happened to the treasures."

"Seems obvious enough," said Andy. Karen was touched by the transfigured look on his face. Andy had always believed in the treasure. It seemed likely that it would turn out even more wonderful than he had dared to dream. It was lovely. She felt so glad for him.

There was a loud knock on the front door. Not an ominous wolf-man's knock. "This'll be Max!" Andy cried, relieved.

He ran to unbar the door. Karen strained her ears eagerly for Max's voice. But she could hear only Andy's, calling across the dark garden in a puzzled tone: "Who's there? Hi! Who's there?"

They hurried to join him. He stood in the open doorway, peering out. He shouted once more, then turned and barred the door again.

"Someone's left a note." He held up a folded piece of paper. They moved back to the lamplit kitchen. "It's addressed to *me*," he said in a surprised tone. He gave a little gasp as he began to read it aloud.

*Mr Vandyke Junior is safe and will return when suitable arrangements have been agreed. Do not inform the police. This would complicate matters and might have bad effects upon Mr Vandyke's health. You may inform his grandfather and warn him to consider seriously any communication he receives from us. He too must speak of this matter to no one else.*

"This is a kidnap note," said Don Angeli gravely. "It is not signed?"

"No."

"It would not be."

Karen could see that the note was in neat block capitals.

"I think this is from Il Barone himself," the priest went on. "I can imagine no one else. Normally it would be typewritten. But he was in a hurry – this is a page from a note-pad, he could not wait to have it typed, so he printed it – he knew that handwriting would give him away. It was urgent to let you know your friend was safe—"

"Safe!" cried Donna Margherita scornfully. "*That* devil!"

"For obviously he did not want you to start searching the hills – and then running to the police. At all costs he wanted to keep them out of it."

"So I gather." Andy still sounded dazed – appalled, as Karen was. "But how did he get hold of Max? And why?"

"Your friend must be important? Or his grandfather?"

"I think the family is well-off—"

Karen felt it was time to tell them all she knew. "Old Mr Vandyke is a multimillionaire."

That last word astounded her two friends more than the priest. Her cousin burst out, almost resentfully, "Karen! You never told *me*!"

"I couldn't tell anybody. I wasn't supposed to know. It was that ghastly creep at the hotel – the man in reception."

She told them how angry Max had been when he was identified from the magazine photograph.

"I was so sorry for him. He didn't want us to know. For once in his life he'd managed to be just one of a gang. He'd have been afraid we'd start treating him differently. It seemed better not to let him know I'd overheard anything. And not tell even you. Sorry."

"You don't have to be sorry." Julie squeezed her arm. "You were dead right."

"Course you were," said Andy.

Yesterday's encounter in the bank explained everything. The receptionist, eager like so many others to curry favour with Il Barone, had passed on the exclusive information that the Vandyke grandson was in the district.

"It would be of great interest to him," said the priest. "It was here in Calabria, some years ago, that the young Getty was kidnapped and held to

148

ransom."

"I've heard about that," said Andy.

Karen felt a sudden choked sensation. "Did he escape?" she managed to say.

Don Angeli hesitated. "He *was* . . . finally . . . released. But at a price."

"The Gettys paid the ransom?"

"It was not money only . . ." Again the priest paused.

"Didn't they cut off the poor bloke's ear or something?" Andy blurted out. And then, seeing Karen's face, looked as if he would rather have bitten off his tongue than said it.

Karen felt Don Angeli's arm round her shoulder. "We must think very calmly," he said, "before we do anything."

# FIFTEEN

Max hoped fervently that it would not be a long drive. He was acutely uncomfortable, folded into that stuffy space, hands bound behind him, unable to move even his legs more than a few inches.

Where were these men taking him? What did they want?

Their leader, who spoke English, had known his name. There was something alarming about that. Worse still, he had added the word "Junior" – so he knew that there was a "Mr Vandyke Senior". In which case he probably knew more than just Grandfather's name. He knew *about* him.

Back home, Max had learnt that children and grandchildren of multimillionaires had to be extra careful. They were exposed to dangers that other young people scarcely thought of. Grandma had quite a thing about kidnapping. Max had always shrugged it off as another example of her well-meaning but tiresome fussiness.

Now, though . . . Well, things *did* happen in Italy. He'd read somewhere that Calabria especially was the happy hunting-ground of kidnappers. Suddenly the childhood bogey became unpleasantly real.

The car pulled up. Someone got out. Low voiced. The leader was muttering instructions. Then the door slammed, footsteps faded down the road, the car drove on again.

Surely, thought Max indignantly, they could have let him travel in normal comfort? He was unarmed, utterly helpless. What were they afraid of? Soon he understood.

The car's speed diminished to a crawl. At frequent intervals the driver hooted impatiently. There were background noises – laughter, a babble of voices, an outdoor radio blaring. They were nosing their way through a village. That was why they had not wanted him to be visible.

He struggled to drum with his feet, but his signals must have been lost in the surrounding hubbub. The village could have been only a small place, for its noises soon fell away behind them. The car gathered speed, changing gear as it began to climb. There were numerous sharp bends, awkward for a helpless captive flung to left or right. He had no idea how far they had travelled or how much time had passed.

If they were heading into the Sila even ten miles would take them into the wilds.

The car swung left, giving him a crack on the head. The surface grew rougher, the driver reduced speed. At last they stopped. Doors opened, footsteps came round to the rear, there was a click of a catch. Suddenly the stars were glittering overhead and the fresh air rushed in with the resinous fragrance of pinewoods.

They heaved him out. His cramped legs buckled under him as they touched the ground. They hauled him upright, steadying him until he could stand. The leader rapped out a terse order. Max let out a yelp as the surgical tape was torn roughly from his wrists.

"I know you will behave yourself, Mr Vandyke. There is really nowhere to run to. You will need your hands to climb these steps. After taking all this trouble I should not like you to break your neck." The man laughed, but not in a particularly pleasant way.

Now that his eyes were adjusted to the starlight, Max saw that the car had stopped in a forest clearing beneath a tall tower. A steep flight of steps went up to a doorway above their heads. As they helped him to climb he was glad of a steadying hand. The steps were crumbly and uneven, badly worn by time.

There were more steps inside. A powerful torch-beam flashed upwards and revealed them spiralling away into the gloom. He remembered a Welsh castle he had recently visited with his grandparents.

One of the men lit a hurricane-lamp to provide a steadier light. They took the climb slowly. Max was faint with hunger. His picnic lunch now seemed a lifetime away. They reached a heavy, nail-studded door. A key turned. They entered a curved room with narrow apertures like the arrow-slits in the Welsh castle.

"Sit down, Mr Vandyke. I am sorry that for the moment there are only these stools." The leader took one himself and Max saw no point in refusing. "Your visit was quite unplanned, but we can soon make better arrangements for your comfort – in case you are here for any length of time." He must have noticed Max's glance at the arrow-slits, for he went on, "In daylight you will be able to see in all directions. This is one of our ancient watch-towers against the Saracen raiders. It is still called the Saracen Tower."

Max's usual interest in history was not uppermost at this moment.

"Who are you?" he demanded. "Why have you brought me here?"

He was fairly sure of both answers. He had not himself seen Il Barone in the bank yesterday, but this self-assured, dapper little man matched Karen's description. And now that the two attendant thugs had removed their wolf-masks he recognized the bigger one as the hefty scoundrel who had stood watchful at the door of the bank when he left.

"It is unnecessary for you to know my name," said the leader smoothly, "and it may be safer for you." Max was thankful that he had restrained his impulse to exclaim that he knew anyhow. Maybe it *would* be safer to pretend complete ignorance.

"As to the reason for bringing you here . . ." The man drew a note-pad from his pocket and uncapped his pen. "I shall need a private telephone number so that I can contact your grandfather."

So, it was as he had feared. A kidnap job.

Max dictated his grandfather's home number. No point in refusing. They could discover it anyhow.

"I have never before conducted such a negotiation," said Il Barone pleasantly. "It is interesting

153

to try something new. I should not have troubled
– I have other very pressing business at this time –
but the opportunity offered itself. I did not know
you were in this region – until yesterday I did not
even know that you existed – and then tonight, to
see your face in my headlights!" He laughed.
"When Fate offers such opportunities it would be
ungrateful to refuse them. Indeed, dangerous.
One must not insult Fate."

I mustn't let him see how scared I am, thought
Max desperately. He said, as calmly as he could,
"Your fate may not be so good if you don't take
me back. My friends will be wondering – they'll
raise the alarm—"

"I have warned them not to."

"You've told them? Already?" Max's jaw
dropped. "But how did you know—"

"I learned today that Donna Margherita had
some young foreigners in her house. That tiresome old woman! She gets in my way – the other
pressing matter I spoke of. I wanted her out
before the end of the month."

Later, thinking everything over during the long
hours of solitude, Max recalled that the opening
of the dam was fixed for the first of September.
Was there a connection? Just then, though, he
was more concerned with his own predicament.

"You've told them already?" he repeated
incredulously.

"I sent one of my men at once with a note. They
will have it by now."

Il Barone's flair for organization seemed to be
all that Don Angeli had said it was. At least he

had given no hint that he knew about the treasure-hunt. Certainly, if he had known of their success, he would not be sitting here now. He would have been down in the valley with a gang of men, digging frantically by torchlight, and by dawn Alaric's hoard would have been spirited away.

For himself, at this moment, Max would have cheerfully bartered away that hoard to be free, unharmed, and on a plane to America. But he pulled himself together. The secret wasn't his to give away. Even if Il Barone let him go in return – and how far could you trust such a man? – he owed it to Andy and the others. He must keep his mouth shut about Alaric.

Il Barone was talking. "It seemed best to tell your friends quickly. I do not want Carabinieri swarming all over the countryside. Also, your friends will be a direct link with your eminent grandfather. They are on the spot, they can assure him that I am not bluffing when I tell him you are in my hands. He will be more ready to negotiate."

"You don't know my grandfather. You're kidding yourself if you think you'll get ransom money out of him."

Il Barone smiled. "Relatives are often very defiant – at first. But as the weeks pass, and all their efforts get nowhere, they begin to soften. In the end the kidnapper wins." He laughed softly. "You see, he always has an ace to play."

"An ace?"

"I promise you, my boy – if I am forced to play the ace it will be done as gently and kindly as possible. If it were possible I would summon the finest surgeon from Naples. But alas, some trifling scruple would prevent him – some silly little point of professional etiquette."

"Professional . . . etiquette?"

"It would not permit him to remove a perfectly healthy human ear." Max let out a gasp of horror and then could only stare at him in appalled silence. "I can overcome that difficulty," Il Barone continued reassuringly. "I have a very skilful man. Only a butcher, true, but *very* skilful. And really the kindest of men."

He stood up and walked to the door. "Once the relatives receive the little package," he said, "they cannot wait to get their loved one into a proper hospital."

# SIXTEEN

Don Angeli stayed that night at Donna Margherita's. They sat for hours round the table, anxiously discussing the situation. Nero curled up on Karen's lap. She found it soothing to stroke his thick fur while they talked, feeling his warm weight through her threadbare jeans.

Ought they to disobey Il Barone and go straight to the police?

The old priest was quite ready to mount his motorcycle and go charging off to Cosenza, but he pointed out that nothing would be gained by such hasty action. "No harm will come to your friend tonight. Indeed, they will take the greatest care of him – so long as there is any hope of getting a ransom."

That was some comfort.

"In the morning," he went on, "I think, yes, you should go straight to the Carabinieri. They wage constant war against the Honourable Company. But – I warn you – they do not always win. They operate under such difficulties. The peasants are in terror of men like Il Barone – they dare not tell the police what they know. And if Max has been taken into the Sila it is full of hiding-places. To search it thoroughly would require an army."

He looked round their dejected faces. "But it is not for me to decide, or for you. It is for his family. Can you get into touch with them?"

Andy pulled out his notebook. "I've got his

grandfather's phone number." Thank goodness, thought Karen, Andy was so conscientious about such things. They looked upon him as the leader of the party and he had listed all home addresses in case of emergency.

"Then tomorrow," said Don Angeli, "you should consult him."

"I will. Soon as I can get to a phone in the morning."

"It'll still be the middle of the night in America," Julie reminded him. She regularly called her parents in Australia and had to remember about time variations.

"True," said the priest. "It is not wise to give a man of his age a sudden shock like this."

Karen calculated that Don Angeli must be almost as old as Mr Vandyke. She could not imagine *him* not rising to an emergency, whatever the hour, but of course he was quite right. To be wakened by such news might give Mr Vandyke a heart attack.

They agreed that Don Angeli would ride into Cosenza at dawn and send out a taxi for Andy and Julie, who would wait a little while before making their transatlantic call. They would not go to the police until they had at least tried to make contact with Max's grandfather and obtain his approval.

"And if we can't get him," said Andy firmly, "I'll just have to take the responsibility myself."

Karen would stay at base, keeping Donna Margherita company and ready to handle any more mysterious notes that might be delivered.

Not surprisingly, Karen slept fitfully and got up at first light. Even so, she found Donna Margherita and the priest in the kitchen.

"Are you off already, Father?"

He smiled. "She will not let me start till I have some coffee inside me!" He moved to the door. "I am going a wee step down the road. To the church. I shall say a prayer there."

He did not invite her to go with him. She would have gladly done so. But she checked her impulse. Perhaps he wanted to be alone. Or maybe it wasn't the thing to suggest, as she wasn't a Catholic. Never mind, she told herself, you can pray anywhere. Even standing by the kitchen-table while Donna Margherita potters at the stove.

How was poor Max faring, she wondered? Where had they taken him, those horrible creatures?

A sound broke in upon her thoughts. A car had pulled up at the gate. What now, for God's sake? *Not* Il Barone? She ran to the foot of the stairs and screamed, "Andy!" She rushed to the front door to bar it until she knew who was coming, but Don Angeli had left it wide open to the morning air. Two uniformed figures were silhouetted against the brightness. Thank God! Carabinieri.

A smiling young officer greeted her in English. "Good morning, *signorina*—"

She gaped at him. "But – how did you *know*?" She could think only of Max's disappearance, which they had not yet reported.

"An American gentleman telephoned yesterday – a Signor Vandyke. About some archaeological

159

discovery."

"Oh, *that!*"

So Max had reached the dam and made his call. Her brain was in a whirl as she wondered how much to say. Andy came rushing downstairs.

"It's the police," she gabbled "Max *had* got through to them – about our find."

Andy got the message. "I'll fetch the stuff." He dashed back to his room for the diadem and the coins. Karen had already taken the two men into the kitchen. After last night's events Donna Margherita seemed more favourably disposed to the forces of law and order. She was pouring them coffee.

They exclaimed at the spendour of the diadem. It flashed in the sunbeams as brightly as when it first adorned the brow of a Roman empress.

"And there are other such objects, *signore?*"

There was no point now in holding anything back. The police were taking over. "Lots, we think," said Andy. He described the reaction of the metal-detector. "We thought it best not to disturb the site any more," he said virtuously. "It's a matter for experts now."

"Quite right." The young officer glanced at his notebook. "And you are Maximilian Vandyke? Forgive me, but you do not sound like an American."

"I'm not. I'm British. Do you want my passport—"

"I think I must speak first to Mr Vandyke. Where is he?"

"We must tell them," said Karen. "We can't

wait till we've told his grandfather." She found much comfort in the sight of that smart Carabiniere uniform. She longed to have someone sharing this awful responsibility.

"Of course," said Andy. "It's out of our hands now." He turned back to the officer, whose face had taken on a keenly interested expression. "We don't *know* where Mr Vandyke is. He went to telephone your people. He never came back. After a few hours this was pushed under the door." He held out the note.

"*So!*" The officer let out a deep breath as he scanned it.

"Don Angeli says it is from this man they call Il Barone."

"He does? I wonder. If it is, this is a new extension of his activities." He explained briefly to his colleague, then said to Andy: "It must have been very soon after your friend spoke to me from the dam."

"Yes, you can pretty well pin-point the time."

"I must report this at once—"

"A pity the phone here has been cut off!"

"We have radio in the car. I will report the disappearance of your friend. Then, as I am here, I had better see the place where you made this discovery. We shall have to post a guard until we can get experts. It is going to be a busy day," he said with wry humour.

At that moment Don Angeli walked in. The two Carabinieri greeted him like an old friend. The priest had caught the end of the conversation.

"I think you will be needing some other experts too – of quite a different kind."

They all looked at him, intrigued by his tone. Julie had just come downstairs and joined the group. Don Angeli smiled grimly round at them, almost enjoying their mystification.

"I have just come from the church. There is a pile of little bags concealed at the foot of the bell-tower. I did not like the look of them. When you radio your headquarters I suggest that you ask them to send an expert in explosives."

"Explosives?" The officer was shaken out of his calm.

"On September the first," said the priest, "the Minister is coming to open the dam. But there is a whisper going through the countryside that the ceremony will never take place. Il Barone has vowed it. So his honour is at stake."

"I had better go down to the church. If you will show me, Father." As the officer started for the door he said with a resigned smile, "It is going to be even busier than I thought, this day."

They all followed him, even Donna Margherita, setting down the coffee-pot with a despairing shrug.

Even at this moment of high drama Julie, being Julie, could not help whispering to Karen as they went, "Isn't he *gorgeous*?"

Luckily Andy was too far in front to hear.

# SEVENTEEN

It was the longest night Max could remember.

Sleep was almost impossible. Even if he could have forgotten for a moment the horror of his situation – telling himself that it was something that would not, could not happen – sheer physical discomfort would have kept him awake.

There were only the stools to sit on. Eventually he was driven to stretch out on the hard floor, filthy though it was with bird-droppings. Chill draughts blew through the arrow-slits.

There was hunger too. They had left him a half-finished packet of biscuits, a broken slab of chocolate. There had been nothing else in the glove-compartment of the car, Il Barone explained apologetically. "If I had known you were coming—"

"You'd have baked a cake," said Max sarcastically. But the familiar catch-phrase did not register with the Italian. He offered cigarettes and looked incredulous when Max declined them. He promised to return with proper food and comforts for his esteemed young guest.

The key had turned in the door, the footsteps faded on the stairs. Max had heard the car start and go humming away into the distance.

He knew he had not been left alone. Il Barone had made that very clear. Even if Max had been an expert lock-picker and could have opened that massive door, he would have found an armed guard waiting below.

The arrow-slits, of course, offered no way of escape. Even wider openings that he could squeeze through would have been no help. He remembered his glimpse of the tower from outside. Its bare masonry offered about as much handhold as a lighthouse. And this room must be almost at the top.

He rationed his scanty food supplies. He had his watch. One biscuit every hour, then one bite from the chocolate slab.

The pale grey dawnlight came. He pressed his face into the arrow-slits. From every opening he saw a rolling wilderness. Treetops, scrub, mountain pasture, the glint of a distant lake . . . But of human habitation not a sign. This then must be the famous Sila.

He had no taste for picturesque scenery just now. The wide views only underlined the utter remoteness of the tower. High though it stood, the pines clustered so densely round it that only this upper storey would peep above the treetops.

Pink sky filled one of the openings. So the east lay in that direction. The information was of little help. On all sides the landscape looked much the same, a grand but rather terrifying solitude. There were endless miles for search-parties to cover.

Still his captors did not return. He finished his last biscuit. He was desperately thirsty.

Then, as the pink light changed to gold, he heard a car for the first time. That showed how far he must be from main roads. The sound stopped just below. The thickness of the wall made it impossible to see the ground at the foot of the tower, but there were footsteps now mounting the stairs.

Would this be Il Barone? On no account, he reminded himself, must he reveal that he knew the man's identity, or they would never dare to let him go. Even if they got the ransom money they would not honour the agreement. He would be returned to his family, yes, but not in a condition to talk and tell his story.

The key turned. Il Barone entered, suave, smelling of after-shave, full of apologies. Three of his men crowded in behind him, laden with assorted burdens.

A card-table was unfolded, a wicker picnic-basket opened, a table-napkin respectfully spread, a bowl filled with steaming soup from a thermos flask. Max did not wait for the spoon. He raised the bowl to his lips and gulped at the scalding liquid.

Il Barone took a stool opposite and beamed benevolently. "I need not wish you 'good appetite'!"

Max did not try to answer. He had grabbed a roll and was devouring it.

"We were delayed. There were Carabinieri everywhere. We had to make a detour to avoid a road-block. I fear that your friends ignored my warning not to tell the authorities."

"I'm glad they did!"

"Do not rejoice too soon. I am not afraid of their finding you. The Sila is a big place. And we can move you constantly if it seems advisable."

"Then why didn't you want the police told?"

"They may upset our negotiations."

"How do you mean?"

"Your family may be willing enough to pay the ransom, but the police may forbid them. For the police it is a logical attitude. They wish to put down all this kidnapping. They say that every time a ransom is paid, people are encouraged to kidnap someone else. If no ransoms were paid, kidnapping would cease. There would be no money in it."

"Sure, that's logical enough."

"But hard on those already kidnapped. If the police are unable to find them. Which often happens."

"I can see that," said Max with sincere feeling.

"Do not worry! One can find ways of getting round police instructions."

"My grandfather is a law-abiding man. He has great respect for the police." Max said this with rather less enthusiasm than he would have done normally.

Il Barone remained optimistic. "He is very rich. One does not become so rich if one has too much respect for the law."

" I guess you don't know my grandfather."

"Alas, no. But I am sure that he is a devoted grandfather – *and* a skilful man of business. He will find ways, never fear. A discreet payment, perhaps, into a Swiss bank account. He may hesitate, of course. We may have to frighten him – just a little – to hurry things up, to show that I too am a man of business. I should be sorry . . ." Il Barone's voice indicated intense regret.

Max tried not to let his mind dwell on the possible ways in which pressure on his family could be increased.

He continued to eat, but more mechanically now. It was a good meal they had brought him. Ham and cold chicken, salad in a plastic box, coffee in another thermos flask.

"When you go home," said Il Barone, "I hope you will be able to speak well of your treatment." His men had set up a deck-chair and a camp-bed equipped with pillows and a duvet. At the far side of the room they had placed discreetly what looked like a camper's chemical toilet. "I have tried to think of everything," he said, "but this is a novel experience for me."

"And me," said Max emphatically.

"I wish Mr Vandyke to realize that he has been dealing with a gentleman – one, indeed, who is highly respected in this region, which unfortunately is the very reason why I cannot divulge my name."

This really bugs him, thought Max with sardonic amusement. He's so *vain*. He'd love to be able to talk to Grandfather on equal terms, one tycoon to another.

As if to confirm this, Il Barone went on in a wistful tone, "One day perhaps – when all this is satisfactorily behind us – you will receive a harmless postcard with good wishes and memories of a holiday encounter in Calabria. You will not know the signature, but you will guess that the name is mine." He laughed softly, pleased with his idea. "In the law court such a document would not be evidence of anything. But it would make an elegant ending to this affair."

He stood up. "You will excuse me. There will be one of my men always close at hand. And of course there will be Goering." He murmured something to the big man, who hurried downstairs. "You had better meet Goering. I call him after Hitler's famous marshal because he too is heavily built – and can be rough with anyone he dislikes. And the name fits the noise he makes. *Grrrh!*" he growled, and laughed at the excellence of his imitation.

The big man returned, almost hauled up the stairs by the dog whose chain he held. Goering was a massive though not enormous beast, black with brown hindquarters, looking as if he weighed about half a ton. Max had seen plenty of Rottweilers. Some of his grandfather's friends kept them as guard-dogs, but Grandfather would have none of them. "I don't want a killer around," he said, "not just to protect property."

At a nod from Il Barone the dog was taken away. "I introduce you to Goering," he explained, "so that you are not tempted to do anything foolish. You might stand behind the door when you heard your meal coming – you might think that you could hit my man with one of these stools. But you would still have to deal with Goering. He will always be chained at the foot of the stairs. No one can leave this tower without passing him. And nobody *can* pass Goering."

Max felt no wish to make the experiment.

Il Barone waited while the remains of the meal

were cleared away, then he followed his men, locking the door behind him. Max watched in sullen silence. There seemed nothing whatever that he could do.

Alone again, he stretched out thankfully on the camp-bed and pulled the duvet over him. He lay staring up at the decayed-looking old beams overhead. There was still a long day to get through. With nothing to read, he was driven back upon his own thoughts. And he had plenty to think about.

What were his friends doing? And the Carabinieri? Something, obviously – his captor had mentioned a road-block. But had they any clues to what had happened to him after leaving the watchmen at the dam? Would the Carabinieri even suspect that Il Barone was involved? And – suppose they did – might they not be tempted to soft-pedal their efforts? According to Don Angeli this region was rotten with corruption. If there were bent cops back home in the States, Max reflected gloomily, there might be even more in Calabria.

It wasn't the kind of meditation that brought peace of mind. Mercifully the effects of his sleepless night added to the meal. He fell asleep and when he woke the afternoon was well advanced.

Round about now Il Barone, or some go-between, would be putting through a call to Grandfather. He wondered what the old man would say. He could guess what his grandmother would, once she'd got over the first shock. "This is what comes of the boy taking off into nowhere with those crazy young Britishers!" Grandma would be raising hell. She'd tell Grandfather to get on to the American ambassador in Rome, or the White House, or the Pope. Maybe all three.

Thoughts of Grandma led on to thoughts of his future – if any. The two things had always been intertwined. Too much intertwined, he now saw.

"If I get out of this place alive," he murmured.

He would live his life as *he* wanted to, not in the stereotyped pattern of a Vandyke grandson. He'd quit Accountancy and Law. Others could carry on the family's financial empire. He'd switch to History. That was where his heart lay.

Heart? That started him on another line of thinking. Karen. Had he any chance with that girl? He'd sensed her hostility from the beginning of the trip. But she'd been softening towards him these last few days. They really did have a heap of things in common.

If I get out of this place alive . . . He felt a new determination. He pictured Grandma's face if one day he was able to break the wonderful news to her. Only *she* wouldn't see it as wonderful news. Giving up his business studies would seem crazy enough, but – to marry a British nobody! She'd maybe have swallowed the "British" if Karen's dad was a lord or something. But he wasn't. He was a real blue-collared wage-earner, probably with a union card. Not Grandma's type at all.

The long day crawled by. The sun moved round the tower, sending long thin beams of gold through the successive arrow-slits. At last there were no bright strips across the floor and the westward apertures showed rose-coloured sky.

He heard a welcome clink of crockery. The key turned. A wary head was thrust in. Seeing Max humped on the bed, not lurking behind the door with an upraised stool in his hands, the guard entered with a tray.

"*Grazie*." said Max.

"*Prego*."

This meal was not up to the standard of the first. Lumpy stew, prepared by the guard himself, who clearly was no chef. Lumps of bread. An unripe apple.

Max indicated that some kind of a light would be welcome, but the man shook his head decisively. Of course, Max realized, they would not want any sign of occupation shining through the arrow-slits, however remote was the chance of its being observed from outside.

The guard took away the tray. Max had a sketchy wash while he could still see the plastic bowl and pail of water provided. The room grew dark. The arrow-slits showed pale around the walls. Westwards he could see the evening star blazing above the horizon. He lay down again on the bed and eventually sleep came.

He was roused by a lugubrious howl from below. Not a bark, not a warning growl, but a long-drawn lamentation suggesting that Goering was far from happy. Max squinted at his watch. The luminous digits registered twenty past four. It was the moon, not as yet the dawn, that made the arrow-slits stand out so brightly.

He realized that the bed was shivering under

him. The whole place seemed to be swaying. The stripes of moonlight joggled to and fro across the floor.

Once, on vacation in California, he had been in a very slight earthquake, an insignificant tremor but a memorable experience to a little boy. This had the same feel, only the swaying was more pronounced. Of course, Calabria was an earthquake zone.

There was just time for a thought which gripped him with sudden fear. He was high up in a ramshackle old watch-tower that had been built centuries ago, long before those modern building techniques which today could make even a skyscraper safe against even a violent convulsion. The ancient walls seemed to reel around him. Cracks and groans came from far below him.

Later he was to learn that the shock had lasted thirteen seconds. It felt like as many minutes.

Now the floor was tilting. Stools and table slid, the bed folded under him, and he was sent rolling on to the floor. Timber was splintering loudly. Slowly, almost gracefully, the tower was subsiding beneath him. He felt a glancing blow on the head, and lost consciousness.

He came to himself in a whirling haze of dust that filled mouth and nostrils. The whirling steadied. He was in a silvery fog – that was the moonlight, and the fog was clearing as the dust settled. He could see now – by some miracle, he was out of the tower. The pines rose around him. Fresh air surged back into his eager lungs.

The tower had *gone*. Or at least the upper part

in which he had been imprisoned. He was now sprawled on top of a great mound of masonry and rubble, broken tiles and jagged beams, such as he had seen so often in newsreels of disaster. His left arm was pinned under a beam. His watch flashed back the moonlight and, peering at his wrist, he saw that it was still going and that the time was twenty-three minutes past four. He had not been unconscious for long.

He felt no pain, did not seem injured. He could move both legs amid the rubble, he was able to wriggle his arm from underneath the beam. He stood up shakily, struggling for a foothold on that sliding, clattering heap of ruin. He felt firmness beneath him. The lower part of the tower, with its thicker walls, must have survived unshaken. He felt his aching head, winced as he touched it and met the sticky blood matting his hair. Otherwise he seemed unhurt. He slithered down to the firm ground below. He could stand straight now, he could walk, and – thank God! – he could run.

It was high time to do so, though he had no idea which way to go. Close behind him he heard sounds of life – the scrabble of loose stones, the gasps of a man struggling to dig himself out, the whine of the mystified Rottweiler.

Max hoped fervently that both man and dog would take time to free themselves. He raced for the shelter of the pines.

A massive figure loomed from the shadows, arms spread to bar his path. He swerved but misjudged things. A hand seized him and jerked him to a standstill.

"Max!" said Don Angeli.

"Quick . . ." Max was gasping breathlessly. "There's a dog—"

"I have my motorcycle. This way!"

They fled down a broad track between the trees.

"Thank God!" His voice came out like a sob.

"I had a hunch, laddie—"

It was no time for explanations. They could hear the dog and the man racing in pursuit.

Don Angeli ran gamely for a man of his years, but it would be a close thing. Max strained his eyes desperately for a glint of moonlight on metal, but the priest had hidden his machine carefully in the undergrowth. "Here!" he cried suddenly in triumph. He wheeled it into view, hitched up his habit and straddled his mount. At the first kick the engine roared into life. "Hang on tight!" he shouted.

Goering was streaking through the trees like a black thunderbolt. Max jumped on behind Don Angeli, gripped for dear life. They were off in the nick of time, racing perilously over the bumpy ground.

A shotgun blazed behind them. They crouched. Max clung hard as they roared on with unslackened speed.

He knew now why Don Angeli was nicknamed "Furioso."

# EIGHTEEN

Karen was beginning to wonder if she would ever get an unbroken night's sleep again.

The earthquake woke them all. The house trembled and swayed giddily. She was reminded of a wild students' party last term. How, next morning, she had tottered out of bed feeling like death.

This time, though, was different. She was all right in herself. It was the room that actually had trembled. It stopped now.

They met Andy outside their bedroom door. "Did *you* . . ." they all exclaimed together.

"Must have been an earthquake," he said. "Happens all the time in these parts. Interesting." It was the geologist speaking. "We're in the zone."

Donna Margherita emerged from her room, very self-possessed, quite different from the night of the wolf-man's visit. She confirmed what Andy said. If earthquakes did not "happen all the time" they were certainly not unusual. Most were slight and did little damage. But her father used to tell her of the terrible one at Messina just before she was born. Eighty-four thousand victims – two-thirds of the city's population!

"If you wish, we can go down to the terrace." She sensed the girls' nervousness.

"Good idea," said Andy. "There's often a second shock soon afterwards."

"You know too much," Julie told him rather acidly.

The girls went to pull on their jeans. Actually the air outside was soft and warm. Nothing looked different. The valley slept in a silver radiance. They felt safer out there where there was nothing to cave in upon them.

Their hostess returned indoors, an uneasy Nero trotting anxiously at her heels. It was Donna Margherita's instinctive reaction to make for the kitchen, throw a handful of dried olive kernels on the glowing ashes, and prepare a pot of coffee.

"Where's Don Angeli?" Julie asked.

"He went off after supper," said Andy. "He'd got a hunch – but he wouldn't say what."

Karen said, "I think he's got an idea where they may be hiding Max. The peasants whisper things to him that they wouldn't tell the Carabinieri. But he doesn't want to raise false hopes, so he didn't tell us anything."

It was no good. However hard they tried, they couldn't get away from the subject of Max's disappearance. They went over and over the scanty facts without coming to any hopeful conclusion.

Don Angeli's discovery in the church had explained some of the other things that had mystified them.

The bags had contained semtex, the terrorist's favourite explosive. Enough, the Carabinieri said, to blow a sizeable hole in the dam and still further delay its official opening.

Who would wish to do a thing like that? The Carabinieri would not commit themselves. They must pursue their inquiries. Don Angeli was more forthcoming: obviously it was Il Barone. He had failed to get the contract awarded to the firm that would have given him a substantial cut from the profits, so he must demonstrate to the world that it did not pay to thwart him. He had obstructed the work as long as he could. Now, when at last it was completed and the Minister coming from Rome to perform the opening ceremony, he would play his trump card.

This, the priest argued, must be why the wolf-man had been sent to frighten Donna Margherita away. Her house was too close to his cache of explosive which he wanted to leave hidden in the church until the last moment. He wanted no possible witness – even a harmless old woman – still living only a stone's throw away.

It all sounded very convincing, but it did not help to answer the question that most concerned them: where was Max?

The friends felt so helpless. They were just spectators now. The Carabinieri had the case in hand and spoke of bringing in troops to scour the region. Grandfather Vandyke had been informed. Andy said that he sounded marvellously cool and competent on the line from America. He was shocked but not shattered. He was waiting to hear from the kidnappers. Meanwhile he was in touch with all the right people.

"And pulling all the right strings," Andy assured the girls. "Take it from me, a man like that knows which strings to pull."

Karen hoped he did. But what strings, she

wondered dejectedly, stretched as far as the mountains of Calabria?

They must decide soon whether to remain here with Donna Margherita or move back into Cosenza where they could be in close touch with Mr Vandyke by telephone. They were reluctant to leave the old woman alone after all she had done for them. Perhaps Andy could hire a bicycle in the town and ride in each day to make a regular transatlantic call? They were certainly not returning to the hotel with that highly dubious receptionist. Karen's own instinct was to stay here. This was where Max would make for if he managed to give his captors the slip.

Barely was the sun above the skyline when this instinct seemed to be justified. They heard the priest's motorcycle, and then, coming up the path, not only his voice but that of their vanished friend.

"*Max!*"

They all rushed out, almost delirious in their relief.

"Ow!" he cried out in pain. In all the confused embracing Karen's arm must have caught the side of his head. She too exclaimed as she saw the dried blood dark on his matted hair.

"Oh, Max! What have they *done* to you?"

"Just a b-bang." he said faintly. "I . . . I'm OK."

He was stammering as though still dazed. Later she felt almost sure that in the heat of the moment they had kissed full on the lips. Or had she dreamt that? It had been so wonderful to see him safe.

178

Julie, always practical, brought a bowl of water and dabbed his head, very gently wiping away the blood and the dust and grit. Karen stood by, feeling useless and suddenly jealous.

"I don't think it's much," said her cousin cheerfully. "It's not deep. But you may feel pretty crook for a while. Best show it to a doctor, soon as we can get you into town."

"We should do that immediately in any case," said Don Angeli. He too sounded dead beat. "The police will want him safe with them in Cosenza. Perhaps I should not have brought him back here – I should have taken him straight into the town. But to tell the truth I was afraid—"

"Afraid?" cried Andy.

"Afraid that the laddie might not hold out those extra miles. He had to hang on behind me on the motorcycle. I knew he had been hurt in the earthquake – and – you see for yourself . . ."

The girls had helped Max to a chair. He was leaning heavily over the kitchen table. Donna Margherita had produced a white cloth as bandage and was now preparing more coffee.

"I will go on now to Cosenza," said the priest. "I will bring back the Carabinieri. And a car—"

"Not till you have had some food," said Donna Margherita sternly. "You have been out all night. You will not remember – you are now an old man. You need not also be an old fool!"

"Very well," he said meekly and sat down.

Karen remembered that these two had once been children in the same village.

"Five minutes only," said Don Angeli, making

an effort to reassert his authority. "We are not safe yet. I shall be happy only when we reach the Carabinieri." He gulped his coffee, and the colour crept back into his grey cheeks. The others could not restrain their eager questions.

"I thought at once of the old watch-tower," he explained. "I had no proof, but I always suspected that Il Barone sometimes made use of it for his schemes. He will not again," he said with grim satisfaction, and told them how it had collapsed in the earthquake.

Karen looked at Max in horror. "And *you* were locked up in the top of it? Lucky you weren't killed!"

"The guard was just as lucky – and that brute of a dog. They'd be at the *bottom* of the heap."

"The lower walls would be much thicker," said Don Angeli. "Perhaps they still stand. It might be only a question of digging a way out through the rubble."

"They sounded OK when they came chasing after me," said Max. "My, was I glad to see Don Angeli!"

The priest set down his empty cup decisively. "I go now." He pulled himself to his feet.

"Couldn't *I* go?" said Andy. "You must be all in. I can ride a motorbike."

Don Angeli smiled but shook his silvery head. "Not this one, I think. She obeys only one master." He moved towards the door, then stopped, finger upraised, with a look of dismay. "I should not have stayed. Listen!"

It was Max who knew the sound. "That's Il Barone's car!"

Donna Margherita laid her hand on his arm. "Upstairs! Hide! We have not seen you, any of us."

Max did not argue. With an obvious effort he staggered out of the kitchen and they heard him heavily mounting the staircase.

Karen sprang to follow him, then checked herself in the nick of time. Il Barone was not troubling with the formality of knocking on the front door. He was on the terrace now, marching in through the open french windows. To run up the stairs would be the surest way to betray Max's line of retreat.

They all came together in the hall. There were three tough-looking characters behind Il Barone. Two carried sawn-off shotguns at the ready. The third – whom she recognized from that incident at the bank – was struggling to restrain an excited Rottweiler on a leash.

Il Barone's eyes flickered from face to face.

"Where is the young Mr Vandyke?" His tone was quiet suave but loaded with menace.

Donna Margherita sailed forward. She let forth a stream of outraged – and probably outrageous – Italian. Her stance and manner were those of a grand lady challenging some impudent intruder in her home. Her vocabulary, Karen suspected, was earthy, pungent and quite possibly obscene. In this moment of crisis the old woman had reverted to the high-spirited peasant girl she had been all those ages ago – the village virago, denouncing her enemies at the public fountain.

Il Barone listened with cynical amusement. He murmured something to the man with the dog. Karen caught the word "garden". The man went out. She heard the swift padding of the Rottweiler's feet as it went racing down into the garden. Good, she thought, they won't find Max there.

Donna Margherita was still in full flow. At last Il Barone lost patience. He gave a curt order to the pair with the shotguns.

"*No!*" snarled the old woman. As they moved forward she sprang on to the bottom stair, arms spread to bar their way. A murderous-looking kitchen knife flashed in her hand.

Il Barone was holding something too. A pistol, small and neat as himself. With his empty hand he motioned to her to stand aside.

She did not budge. She had become a tigress. She launched into another defiant tirade. It sounded as though she were reminding him that the Honourable Society did not make war on women. He laughed. He raised his pistol, ordered her brusquely to get out of the way.

She held her ground. Her face was convulsed with fury, she brandished the knife at him, in her vibrant voice she was clearly telling Il Barone what she would do with it if he came a step nearer.

The shotgun men were edging forward. With sudden alarm Karen saw that Andy too had taken a pace or two as if to intervene. Her own vision was for a moment or two obstructed and she did not see exactly what happened next.

She heard the dry crack of the little pistol.

Donna Margherita's tirade ceased abruptly. Every one rushed forward. Karen saw then that the old woman had crumpled into a black heap across the foot of the staircase.

"*Dio mio!*" Even Il Barone joined in the chorus of horror. He was on his knees beside her, pouring out protestations of innocence. "Don Angeli!" he called. Then, looking round, he shouted urgently to the others in English. "Where is Don Angeli? She must have a priest!"

There was no sign of him. From the road outside came the roar of a motorcycle bursting into life. Even as Karen grasped its significance it was fading rapidly into the distance.

# NINETEEN

"You've killed her!" screamed Julie, dropping to her knees beside Donna Margherita.

"Never!" protested Il Barone. "I swear to God, I did not harm her."

He crossed himself devoutly. Only afterwards did Karen think to herself, how odd, this piety in such a thorough villain. "Look," he went on earnestly, "no blood – not a drop of blood! Put your hand here, signorina. Can you feel her heart? No? It was an attack of the heart. She was so old—"

"Well, *you* frightened her," said Julie unrelenting. "You're a murderer just the same."

"No, never, *signorina*—"

One of the men stepped forward, said something in Italian, and pointed up the staircase. Il Barone exclaimed in triumph and relief. He pointed too.

"You see, all of you?"

On the wall was a bullet-hole, the plaster cracked around it. Even when Donna Margherita was standing upright it would have been well above her head.

"It doesn't make much difference," said Andy dourly.

They all looked sadly down at her. There seemed no doubt that she was dead. None the less, Julie insisted on trying the kiss of life, so they lifted her gently from her crumpled position and laid her flat. Il Barone and his men watched Julie's efforts, at first with interest, then with impatience.

"You waste time," said Il Barone. "No good. I tell you, she was so old."

Outside in the garden the Rottweiler could be heard snarling ominously. The man with him was shouting. At a word from their leader the men with shotguns went pelting up the staircase. Il Barone drew his pistol again and covered the young people.

"You will please not move, any of you. If I shoot again, I shall not shoot to miss." He sounded as if he meant it. "I know that Mr Vandyke is upstairs. He was just now climbing out of a window. When he saw my man in the garden – and the dog – he changed his mind."

It was hopeless, of course, thought Karen despairingly. There couldn't be anywhere much to hide, upstairs. And if Max had dropped from the window . . .

She shuddered. These men didn't want to kill him, not while there was any chance of collecting ransom, but there was that terrifying dog to reckon with. The dog didn't understand the value of money.

Here was Max, coming downstairs, a shotgun poked into the small of the back. He managed a weak smile at his friends. "Too bad I couldn't make it . . ." Then, for the first time, he saw Donna Margherita stretched out on the floor. Her face was covered with the immaculate white handkerchief that Il Barone had whipped out of his breast pocket. "Oh, God!" he said chokingly, stopped, but the men shoved him forward remorselessly.

"We have wasted too much time," said Il Barone. "That accursed priest has slipped away." He must have seized his chance, thought Karen, when all eyes were riveted on Donna Margherita delivering her harangue from the foot of the stairs. It could never have occurred to him that she would be in real danger herself, when the Honourable Society had its code against harming women.

"It will not take him long to Cosenza," Il Barone continued, "the mad speed he rides. We shall soon have the Carabinieri—" He broke off and issued terse instructions to his men.

The three friends could only stand there helplessly. One of the men had turned to cover them with his shotgun. The other kept his weapon menacingly pressed against Max.

Could Don Angeli bring help in time? Karen remembered the miles of road to the town. She remembered something else that had not registered at the time amid all the hubbub.

The noise of the receding motorcycle . . . It had been different. It had not been the usual full-throated roar of the machine surging up the hill and over the crest on its way to the main road. It had started as explosively as usual, but changed quickly to an effortless hum that had faded in moments.

It must have been going *down* the hill.

It had never sounded like that before when Don Angeli left them. He never rode downhill, because the road led nowhere – it ended at the bottom of the village. Then there were only the fields, the boulder-strewn river, the mule-track slanting up the opposite hillside to the other road across the valley. Not even Furioso could ride his motorbike to Cosenza that way.

He must have remembered something that she had forgotten. Yesterday, when the lieutenant had come out – only twenty-four hours ago, though it seemed like a week – he had promised to post a guard over the site of their discovery. There should be someone there now.

She prayed fervently. If only she could delay Il Barone's departure for even a few minutes . . .

She spoke out boldly. "Mr Vandyke hurt his head in the earthquake. It needs attention – we were going to take him to a doctor. Will you at least let us dress the wound before you take him away again?"

Il Barone laughed roughly. "We are used to wounds. We can do whatever is needed. When we get him to a safe place." He turned and said something to one of his men. About starting the car, she thought.

The men went out, pushing Max in front of them. She heard the other one, with the dog, join them outside the door.

Their leader still covered the friends with his pistol. His eyes roved warily from one to another, dwelling mainly on Andy with his formidable physique.

"I will not waste time having you tied up or locked away. You can come out and wave goodbye

187

to your friend if you choose." He had recovered his old arrogant confidence. He was completely relaxed. "Even if you run after us and throw stones like a village boy," he told Andy amusedly, "you will not get far. My car is very high-powered – and the hill is very steep!"

He shepherded them out in front of him. The car was still facing down the road. One man was in the driving seat, struggling desperately to start the engine. Il Barone shouted impatiently. The man called back. Karen caught the name "Furioso".

Il Barone lost his calm and swore. "That damnable Don Angeli! He has done something to the car. A priest has no business to understand machinery!"

All the men were shaking their heads gloomily. There seemed a unanimous opinion that it was impossible to start the engine. After a brief inspection Il Barone appeared to agree.

He turned to Max. "I fear you must walk, Mr Vandyke. We take to the hills. Not for the first time." To Andy he said sharply. "Take off your shoes. Quickly!" He took the shoes and hurled them down the garden. They sailed away in a great arc and vanished with a crackle of branches. "Now you cannot run after us very far. The girls also." He grabbed Julie's trainers and sent them hurtling into the prickliest bushes. "Not you," he told Karen, "you will be more useful—" He shouted to his men, a new note of warning in his voice.

He gripped Karen's arm and twisted it so that she cried out in pain. He propelled her across the road, past the useless immobilised limousine and on to the scrubby hillside beyond. Max and his escort were just in front. The other two men, with the dog on leash, brought up the rear.

Andy and Julie started gamely in pursuit, braving the shotguns that were levelled at them from time to time. But what could they do, Karen thought despairingly? They were unarmed and barefoot on the sharp-edged stones. They could not keep up for long.

Indeed, they had stopped already. They were waving and pointing urgently with outstretched arms. Their desperate voices rang across the empty valley. Turning her head again, in spite of Il Barone's tightened grip as he strove to bustle her faster up the mountainside, she saw that her friends were facing *down* the slope, away from her.

They were calling to a little line of figures hurrying up behind them. Uniformed figures – Carabinieri! Barring one, the tallest, who wore the habit of a priest.

Don Angeli could not match the swift pace of those younger men. But neither could Il Barone, a puffy middle-aged man in elegant city shoes, who had also to keep his grip on her arm and press a pistol against her ribs.

The Carabinieri were gaining steadily. Snatching another glance back, she recognized the good-looking officer whom Julie had privately christened Lieutenant Gorgeous. His men held carbines at the ready as they came surging up the hillside.

Il Barone was labouring under the exertion. He

stopped, his breath coming in great whistling gasps. The pursuers came on until he shouted something and they paused. Only the priest somehow forced himself on until he caught up with them and stood panting at the lieutenant's side.

The pistol muzzle had moved from Karen's ribs and was hard and cold against her temple. Whatever Il Barone was calling down to the Carabinieri it had made them hesitate. Now he was murmuring in her ear.

"If I tell them I will shoot Mr Vandyke they will not believe me. He is still too valuable. They would think I bluff. But if I tell them I will shoot *you*, that is different."

"Of course," she agreed tartly. "There's no money in *me*. I'm expendable." So this was why he had dragged her along. As a hostage.

From the corner of her eye she could see Max, and his guard forcing him roughly up the slope. Soon they would be over the crest and lost to view.

Il Barone was playing for time, to hold back their pursuers while Max was hustled away to some new hiding-place. Then, with Karen as hostage, he would do some deal with the Carabinieri to ensure his own escape. So long as he had her as a shield they would not open fire.

The angry voices rang to and fro. Once the Carabinieri began to edge forward again. Il Barone waved his pistol and held the muzzle at Karen's head. The men stopped. Only one figure came on. Don Angeli. Breathless, stumbling, arms outspread, his face the face of an avenging angel.

Il Barone shouted, threatening. The priest still came plunging on.

He thinks that they would never shoot at a priest, thought Karen. Well, they were not supposed to kill women. But, accidentally or not, Donna Margherita lay dead in the house down the hill.

The pistol was still pressed hard against her temple. While she could feel it, Il Barone could not take aim at Don Angeli. If he moved it away she must be nerved to act. His grip on her right arm never relaxed. Could she make a grab with her left hand and spoil his aim?

Il Barone, however, had another weapon at his disposal. He called to the dog-handler. The man stooped and unleashed the Rottweiler. The beast shot forward like a discharged torpedo, launching himself down the slope.

It was not only the dog that was quick off the mark. Several shots cracked out together. Karen saw the great leap, the black mass flying through the air, Don Angeli knocked backwards by the impact. Then she saw the lieutenant run forward and help the priest totter to his feet. Only the dog lay still.

Firing had become general. The pistol no longer bored into her skin. Il Barone had loosened the grip on her arm. He was shooting at the Carabinieri as they came up the hill.

This was her chance. She ran, ducking and swerving as fast as the rough ground allowed her. She tripped, sprawled in the thorny scrub. She lay still, the breath knocked out of her. The shots echoed back from the mountainside across the valley.

Silence came. Don Angeli was kneeling beside her. "Are ye all right, lass?"

"Yes, I'm OK," she gasped. "Is Max?"

"Ay, he's fine. Just fine."

# TWENTY

In a few moments Max was there to prove it.

"The guy with me just quit," he explained. "I guess he saw how things would work out. He'd more chance of making his getaway if he hadn't got me to drag along."

Karen sat up and looked around her. Il Barone's other two followers had thrown down their shotguns. One was having his arm bandaged. Andy and Julie, still barefoot, were painfully picking their way up the mountainside.

At first she could see no sign of Il Barone. Then she noticed that Don Angeli was kneeling beside a motionless figure, holding up a crucifix, pattering softly in Latin.

Max followed her glance. "That's only a formality, I reckon – he's had it. And I for one shan't go into mourning."

Nor, it soon appeared, would the good-looking lieutenant who had fired the fatal shot.

"It simplifies matters a whole lot," Andy explained later when they could talk things over more calmly. "He was obviously guilty—"

"Guilty as hell," said Max with feeling.

"But he'd have hired the best lawyers, the trial would have dragged on for ever, witnesses would have been threatened – perhaps murdered by the Honourable Society! Even in jail these gang bosses live like princes – they practically run the jail, have the best food and drink sent in to them, and often end by getting off. Anyhow, the lieutenant was shooting in self-defence."

Karen thought of Donna Margherita. She thought of all that Max had gone through, and might have suffered if this affair had turned out differently. She could feel no regret that Il Barone was dead, like his own savage dog. This corner of Calabria would be a freer, safer place.

They all straggled down to the house again. Nero was crouched beside his mistress. He streaked out into the garden as the Carabinieri came clumping in – Karen never saw him again. But when she thought of him in the months that followed she tried to comfort herself with the knowledge that Nero was a survivor.

They carried Donna Margherita upstairs to her bed. Don Angeli placed his crucifix between her cold fingers. As he lifted the corner of the sheet to draw it over her face he bent over impulsively and kissed her.

Karen was the only one to see. They were the last two left in the room. As the priest turned from the bed his face was working with an emotion for once he could not control.

"We had known each other a long time," he explained.

"Since you were children?" she murmured sympathetically.

"Yes. Boy and girl. At that time—" He paused, and smiled down at her. "Some people imagine that priests do not have feelings like other people. But the good God made us all. One must be a man before one can become a priest. And a boy before one can become a man."

They followed the others downstairs. The lieutenant was making efficient arrangements. He sent a man hurrying to the police car to radio for assistance. An ambulance, a van for the two prisoners, a car for the young people . . .

"You will not want to stay here," he said. "We shall take you to a hotel. You will have to make sworn statements about what has occurred, there will be many formalities." He smiled at Julie. "Perhaps, while we wait, you could make some coffee?"

"Sure!" Julie went off to the kitchen, glad of something to do. It would obviously be a little while before the transport arrived.

Surprisingly, however, she had only just brought in the coffee when they heard a vehicle pull up at the gate. At the door was a distinguished-looking old man with a pointed beard and pince-nez dangling on a black ribbon.

"I am Professor Grado," he announced in precise English. "Are you the young people who have made this interesting discovery? It is *most* exciting."

After the grimmer events of the past few hours the word "exciting" came as welcome comic relief. They began to laugh a little hysterically. The lieutenant came forward and hurriedly explained.

It seemed hardly the moment to talk about Alaric's treasure, with Donna Margherita lying dead upstairs. But they could do nothing for her, and this eminent professor had come dashing down the *autostrada* from Naples in the early hours of the morning, and they must answer his eager questions. It was really a relief to have something to do while they waited for the car, and to have an excuse for getting out of this house of death.

"The police are holding the diadem and the coins," Andy explained as they set off.

"But you think that there are other objects?"

"I feel certain. We were using a metal-detector. And considering the lie of the ground – it could easily be the original river-bed – where the Goths buried the king and his treasure."

Professor Grado gave a non-committal grunt. But when they led him across the fields to the roped-off area where the Carabinieri had resumed their guard, his disbelief began to weaken.

"If this is true, my young friend . . ." he said huskily.

"You'll need to work fast," Max warned him. "All this will be under water in a few weeks from now."

"I shall organize the dig immediately."

The professor was not the only one who was busy in the week that followed.

As the lieutenant had warned them, there were many formalities. They had to make sworn statements about the circumstances of Donna Margherita's death and Il Barone's second attempt to kidnap Max. They were all witnesses to the manner of his death in the gun-battle with the Carabinieri. Max had to make a separate statement on his imprisonment in the watch-tower and to identify the two prisoners as among the men who had kidnapped him and held him there.

Besides all these legal procedures there were lengthy telephone conversations with Max's grandparents, who were dissuaded only with difficulty from dashing back across the Atlantic to fetch him. Then there was the American consul from Naples, there were newspaper men and television interviewers.

The kidnapping of a Vandyke was big news. And still the archaeological story had not broken . . .

In their Cosenza hotel they were badgered night and day. They only once had the chance to return to Donna Margherita's house. That was for her funeral.

It was a quiet one. Don Angeli, of course, arranged it. Don Angeli indeed arranged everything. There were difficulties about laying the old woman to rest beside her beloved Sammy. Strictly speaking, there should have been no fresh burials in the evacuated village. "But in Calabria," said the priest with a sad smile, "everything can be fixed." He fixed it.

They did not attend Il Barone's funeral, though they were almost the only people in Cosenza who did not. Thousands of black-suited pious-faced men followed his ornate coffin from the cathedral. The cost of the flowers alone, said Don Angeli dryly, would have fed several poor families for a year.

Meanwhile, Professor Grado had established his camp and begun to dig. After a few days an urgent message reached the friends at their hotel. Would they come out to the site immediately? A car was waiting at the door.

They found the professor in a state of high excitement. Where they had patiently trudged to and fro with the detector, and then pecked so cautiously with their garden tools, the site was transformed with deep trenches, heaps of boulders and mounds of earth.

"You *have* got on!" cried Karen admiringly.

"It was necessary – because of the reservoir. And this morning – I sent for you at once, because you must see what we have found! It must all be taken away to Naples tonight. We dare not keep it here an hour longer than necessary."

He led them to a portable cabin and unlocked the door.

They cried out in unison. The interior was a dull glimmer of unwashed gold and blackened silver. Bowls, goblets, lamps, vases, urns, huge embossed dishes . . .

"And *these*," he announced triumphantly, "can only have come originally from the Temple at Jerusalem!"

They saw before them the seven long silver trumpets of the Jewish priests. They saw the seven-branched golden candelabrum that had once lighted the Holy of Holies. Here was the final proof. They had found the hoard of Alaric.

The next day the pressmen were back in Cosenza. The four friends had to tell and re-tell their story to the cameras and microphones and tape-recorders.

198

Their month had almost run out. Term loomed near for Karen and Andy. Julie had to start her next temporary job in London. The Vandyke family were urging Max to return on the earliest possible flight from Paris.

"I want to get back, myself," he said. "Tell 'em what I've figured out. I know what I want to do now. History. Archaeology, maybe. Your Oxford – or maybe Cambridge."

"That would be lovely," said Karen. But she was not thinking about the attractions of those ancient universities.

Max travelled back in the train with them as far as Paris. Then, in the noisy railway station, came the inevitable goodbyes. "You'll have to shave *this* off before you see Grandma," she teased him as she felt his beard against her face for the last time.

"I don't know that I shall," he said, the new independence more marked than ever in his voice.

The station echoed round them. "We never got to Sicily," she said wistfully.

"Never mind. There'll be another time."

"Maybe." She had made up her mind that there would.

"You got me quite interested in Sicily," he said. "All those Greek temples. And the Roman mosaics."

But she knew, as he kissed her through the window and the train began to glide inexorably out of the station, she had got him interested in much more than mosaics.

# SHADOW UNDER THE SEA

Geoffrey Trease

A hand grabbed the collar of her denim jacket and jerked her savagely to her feet. She found herself looking down the barrel of Shulgin's gun.

In the new Russia of glasnost and perestroika, making friends can be surprisingly easy – as Kate discovers when she meets Stepan and Marina. But the bad old days aren't over yet – not while the sinister Comrade Shulgin is alive and plotting…

"Crime and archaeological discovery and teenage romance are deftly interwoven in this beautifully paced, engrossing story."
*The Times Educational Supplement*

# WHY WEEPS THE BROGAN?

Hugh Scott

WED. 4 YEARS 81 DAYS FROM HOSTILITIES ... so reads the date on the clock in CENTRAL HALL.

For Saxon and Gilbert, though, it's just another day in their ritualized indoor existence. Saxon bakes, Gilbert brushes, together they visit the Irradiated Food Store, guarding against spiders. Among the dusty display cases, however, a far more disturbing creature moves... But what *is* the Brogan? And why does it weep?

"Deftly evoked, the narrative is cleverly constructed, and there is no denying the nightmarish power of the story. There is a true shock ending." *The Listener*

"A very compelling and very interesting book."
*Jill Paton Walsh*
*The Times Educational Supplement*

A Whitbread Novel Award-Winner
Shortlisted for the McVitie's Prize

# SHADOW IN HAWTHORN BAY

Janet Lunn

Fifteen-year-old Highland girl Mary Urquhart has the gift of second sight. One spring morning in 1815 she hears the voice of her beloved cousin Duncan calling to her from three thousand miles away in upper Canada and knows that somehow she must go to him. It is to prove a long and perilous journey, however, and Mary encounters much heartbreak and adversity before her quest finally comes to an end.

"Memorable ... haunting... In one sense this is a ghost-novel – but it is also true to human behaviour."
*Naomi Lewis, The Observer*

"Janet Lunn tells a compelling tale."
*The Times Educational Supplement*

# SECOND STAR
# TO THE RIGHT

Deborah Hautzig

I wouldn't be half bad-looking if I were thin. 5'5½", blue eyes, long light brown hair, small hips – and 125 pounds. If I were thin, my life would be perfect.

On the face of it, Leslie is a normal, healthy, well-adjusted fourteen-year-old girl. She goes to a good school, has a great friend in Cavett, and a mother who loves her to the moon and back. She should be happy, yet she's not. She would be, if only she were thinner. But how thin do you have to be to find happiness?

This is a haunting, honest, utterly compelling account of a girl in the grip of anorexia nervosa.

# DOUBLE VISION

Diana Hendry

"People would do a lot better if they could see double like me... I mean seeing things two ways – with the head and the heart. Reason and imagination."

It's the 1950s and, for fifteen-year-old Eliza Bishop, life in a small, North West coastal town is unbearably claustrophobic. But for her small, fearful sister Lily, the seaside setting affords unlimited scope to her imaginative mind. Through these two very different pairs of eyes a memorable range of characters, events and emotions is brought into vision.

"Succeeds totally where very few books do, as a novel which bestrides the two worlds of adult and children's fiction with total success in both... The stuff of which the very best fiction is wrought."
*Susan Hill, The Sunday Times*

"Full of acute observation and humour."
Geoffrey Trease,
*The Times Educational Supplement*

# THE DREAM THING

Judy Allen

Jen is half-gypsy and illegitimate, and hates it. At school she has to endure mercilesss teasing about her background – even from her friend Tom. When gypsies arrive and set up camp on the wasteland under the flyover, it's the final straw. Then the real hate begins... With it comes the "dream thing" – sharp, disturbing, monstrous, it haunts her nights and takes on an increasingly terrifying reality. But where does it come from?

"A subtle and perceptive portrait of a disturbed mind, a frightening illustration of the powers of unreason."
*The Daily Telegraph*

By the author of the Whitbread Children's Novel Award-winner, *Awaiting Developments*.